Empty Nest

Tales from Grace Chapel Inn 

Empty Nest

PAM HANSON &
BARBARA ANDREWS

Guideposts
New York, New York

Empty Nest

ISBN-13: 978-0-8249-4518-3

Published by Guideposts
16 East 34th Street
New York, New York 10016
www.guideposts.org

Distributed by Ideals Publications, a Guideposts company
2630 Elm Hill Pike, Suite 100
Nashville, TN 37214

Cover art by Deborah Chabrian
Cover by Wendy Bass
Designed and typeset by Müllerhaus Publishing Group | www.mullerhaus.net

Printed and bound in the United States of America
10 9 8 7 6 5 4 3 2 1

Grace Chapel Inn

A place where one can be
refreshed and encouraged,
a place of hope and healing,
a place where God is at home.

Acknowledgments

To Andrew, with love from Grandma and Mom.

Many thanks to Barb Carl for help on Pennsylvania trial procedure. Any errors are ours, not hers. And thanks to Judy Ward for supplying information and inspiration about quilting.

—Pam Hanson and Barbara Andrews

Chapter One

"Cynthia was a bit mysterious about her plans, don't you think?" Louise Howard Smith sat at the kitchen table, sipping tea, preoccupied with thoughts of her daughter's upcoming visit.

"I can't say that had occurred to me," her sister Jane Howard said. "How do you like the almond spice tea? It came in an assortment that I just bought. I can't wait to try all the flavors. How does guava peach sound to you?"

"Ah, interesting."

Louise much preferred traditional flavors like Earl Grey, but she didn't want to discourage her sister's inventiveness. Jane, age fifty and Louise's junior by fifteen years, was the official chef for the Grace Chapel Inn bed-and-breakfast. Without Jane, Louise and their middle sister Alice might never have ventured into the business of inn-keeping.

Although Louise still sorely missed her deceased husband Eliot, her life in Acorn Hill was pleasant and full of interesting challenges. Her one regret was that she and her only child were geographically distant, so she was delighted that Cynthia was coming for a stay. What puzzled her was Cynthia's vague reference to a colleague who would be with her.

"I'm glad she picked April for a visit," Jane said, sitting across from Louise at the kitchen table. "Fortunately, it's a quiet time so we can give both of them a guest room. We're booked solid for most of May."

Jane was reading names on the little packets of tea as she talked, taking different colored foil packs out of a tin box. "Here's one I've never heard of—nettle tea. Nettle sounds like something I would weed out of the garden, not drink. Listen to these: chocolate, caramel, vanilla bean. I wonder if honey lemon ginseng is good."

"Probably better than ginseng alone. The only time I tried it, it tasted like wet newsprint," Louise commented.

"Yum, hawthorn berry," Jane said. "I think I'll try that next."

"I'm always glad to welcome Cynthia's acquaintances, but she was very close-mouthed about exactly who this Joanna Gordon is," Louise said, bringing the conversation back to the topic of the visit.

"I thought you said she worked with Cynthia at the publishing house."

"Yes, that's what Cynthia said."

The Boston publishing firm where Cynthia was a children's book editor was doing extensive renovations on their antiquated offices. Cynthia said it had become impossible to get any work done there. So instead of holing up in her small apartment in order to work, she was bringing a book she was editing, along with a young woman who also worked for the publisher.

"She was probably just busy. I'm sure she didn't mean to be mysterious. Maybe Joanna was in the office with her when she called. That could explain why she said so little about her."

"Yes, that's logical," Louise said, even though she was unconvinced.

"What's logical?"

Alice Howard came into the kitchen dressed in well-worn jeans and a bright-red knit shirt, which contrasted with her rusty-brown hair and warm brown eyes. It also announced that she was on vacation from her part-time nursing job at the hospital in the neighboring town of Potterston.

"Good morning, sleepyhead," Jane said teasingly, although both she and Louise had agreed it was good that their sister was getting some extra rest. Alice had been filling in full time for a nurse who had been taken ill and greatly deserved the two weeks off that she had accrued.

"I feel like a new woman," Alice said, her sparkle belying her sixty-two years. "I can't wait until Cynthia gets here. It seems like ages since she could spend more than a weekend with us."

"That's what we were talking about," Jane said. "Louise thinks there's something mysterious about the woman she's bringing."

"I thought I was the mystery fan in this house," Alice said with a soft chuckle.

"It's just that she said so little about her," Louise explained. "She was even a bit abrupt when I asked about Joanna, and that's not at all like Cynthia."

"I suggested that Joanna was probably in the office when Cynthia called," Jane said.

"That's probably it," Alice agreed.

"Guess what I'm going to do today?" Jane said.

"Paint butterflies on the mailbox?" Alice guessed, remembering Jane's complaint that theirs was looking shabby.

"Make cupcakes for Grace Chapel's shut-in list?" Louise asked, knowing that Jane took a special interest in visiting church members who were no longer able to make it to services.

"Not today," Jane said. "Remember the new bird feeder I bought last week? I'm going to put it up. I just have to decide where to install it."

"Please, not where my piano students can watch it during lessons," Louise said emphatically. "Some of them would be too distracted by the antics of our feathered friends."

"The middle of the garden might be nice," Alice said, "although you might be able to enjoy it more hanging outside the kitchen window."

"I think closer to a window would be best," Jane said thoughtfully. "I want to get it installed today since Cynthia is due tomorrow. I want to make a special dinner to welcome my only niece. In fact, I think I'll pull out some recipes I've been meaning to try. I cook so many breakfasts that doing a special dinner is a treat for me."

"I'm sure Cynthia won't expect a fancy meal," Louise said, although she knew it was impossible to rein in Jane's enthusiasm when she had a reason to go all out with her cooking. Before returning to Acorn Hill, Jane had spent a number of years as head chef in a well-known San Francisco restaurant. There was nothing she enjoyed more than planning and presenting a delicious meal.

"Expect or not, she's getting one," Jane said with determination. "I hope Joanna appreciates good food."

"All I know is that I love my niece, and I'm sure we'll like anyone she brings with her," Alice said. Louise couldn't argue with that, but she was still curious about Joanna. Louise had a strong feeling that there was more to the visit than she'd been told.

Jane was eager to install her new bird feeder, even though she knew the birds could fend for themselves perfectly well in the spring and summer. In winter she would keep it stocked with wild birdseed and suet, which was sure to attract a good variety of the lovely little creatures, but for now she just wanted to see how it would look in its new location.

She decided to put it outside the kitchen window as Alice had suggested. Besides being a wonderful place to view the birds, it was located far enough from tree branches to make it difficult for squirrels to raid. The small animal acrobats were fun to watch as they scurried through the trees at the back of the Howard property, but their voracious appetites left little for the birds if they gained access to the feeder.

The bird-feeder kit was in the gardening shed, and Jane went out to get it as soon as the kitchen was in order. She put the kit, a shovel and a few tools in the lightweight metal cart they used around the lawn and pulled it to the back of the house. The ground was relatively flat, so her challenge was to find a spot where the feeder could be viewed easily. The directions suggested proximity to bushes or trees, but Jane knew how far squirrels could jump, as much as twelve feet through the air when they were determined to get at food.

"Need any help?" Alice asked, walking toward her from the house.

"I'd love some. I was about to inventory the parts," she said, pulling a pole from the box. "If you want to read this list, I'll make sure we have everything."

"Sounds easy enough," Alice said, taking the direction sheet from her sister.

"How many screws are supposed to be here?" Jane asked, pulling out a plastic packet.

"Twenty, it says here."

"Oh dear, I didn't think assembly would be that involved."

"Most of them seem to go in the little wooden shelter at the top that keeps the food clean and dry."

"This is the baffle, I guess." Jane held out a domed metal piece meant to slip over the pole.

"Is that a shield to keep the squirrels from climbing up the pole and stealing the birds' food?"

"Yes. It's amazing what the little rascals can reach."

"I imagine it will discourage Wendell too," Alice said, speaking affectionately of the inn's gray-striped tabby. "Although we've never caught him hunting birds."

"I suspect he's too lazy to hunt when he can get a treat from me just by coming to the kitchen and rubbing against my ankles."

"Do you want me to dig a hole for the pole?" Alice asked.

"I'll do that if you want to install the baffle." Jane brushed aside a lock of dark hair that had escaped her ponytail and pushed the shovel into ground made soft by spring rains.

"This is quite the little mansion," Alice said, studying the pile of wooden pieces on the ground. "What kind of birds do you think you'll attract?"

"I'll be thrilled to get a bluebird or maybe cardinals. I enjoy the little titmice and chickadees—in fact, I enjoy them all, even the sparrows."

"I can never think of sparrows without thinking of one of my favorite Bible verses," Alice said. "'Are not two sparrows sold for a penny? Yet not one of them will fall to the ground apart from the will of your Father'" (Matthew 10:29).

"That verse also comes to my mind when I see a sparrow. It's a very comforting thought."

"You're better at assembling things, and this little house is too complicated for me," Alice said. "I'll stick the pole in the ground and fill the hole with dirt. You can figure out how the house goes together."

"Twenty screws," Jane said, staring at the jumble of wooden pieces. "Maybe I should have waited for Cynthia. She used to love jigsaw puzzles."

"I hope she doesn't have too much work to do. We don't see nearly enough of her," Alice said. "And now I'm curious to meet this mysterious Joanna."

Louise saw her sisters through the kitchen window, hard at work on the bird feeder, but didn't join them because she had something she wanted to do in the guest rooms. Bouquets of spring flowers would be the perfect welcome for Cynthia and Joanna. Louise went to the garden to snip some bright red tulips, pink peonies and some fragrant white lilacs. She arranged them in the kitchen and headed up the stairs to the second floor.

The Sunset Room and the Garden Room at the front of the house were booked, but the two rooms at the rear were equally nice, the only drawback being that they shared a bath.

Louise put the first vase in the Symphony Room, which she planned to give to Joanna. It was a pretty room with a climbing-rose-patterned wallpaper. Cynthia would stay in the Sunrise Room, a room that matched her personality. It had a cheery atmosphere created by the pale blue, creamy white and sunny yellow color scheme. The patchwork quilt on the bed picked up the room's colors, and a large oak-framed landscape contributed to the restful ambiance.

Louise put the flowers on the dresser and fussed about the room for a few minutes, making sure everything was as nice as it could be. She suddenly had a vision of her daughter as she'd been as a child—lively, sweet and imaginative. She'd lived in a world of possibilities, seeing fairies and elves in her family's flower garden and faces in the clouds. Her father had encouraged her with his wonderful store of fables and folktales. It was a tribute to him that she'd made a career as a children's book editor.

This would be her daughter's longest visit in quite some time, and Louise was greatly looking forward to it. While Cynthia was bringing her work, there still would be time for the two of them to catch up. Cynthia loved her life in Boston and enjoyed her job immensely, and Louise was eager to catch up on the news about both.

Perching on the edge of the bed, Louise wondered about Joanna. Her maternal instinct told her that something wasn't quite right.

Her thoughts then turned to a problem of her own, the notice she'd received just before she went out to the garden. She had learned some weeks before that she had been selected to be in the district court's jury pool for this term, but today she had been notified to report on Monday. Being in the pool didn't mean that she would be called to serve on every case during her term of service. It did mean that she had to be available to go to the county courthouse in Potterston whenever she was ordered to appear.

Some people who were on a panel never had to be on a jury. Others might sit on several before their time of service was over. It all depended on the luck of the draw and how busy the court calendar was. Even though Louise had been called to appear, she might not be selected for a trial.

Louise knew that some citizens went to elaborate lengths to avoid serving. They might feign illness or plead urgent family business. She'd heard of more imaginative ways like professing a relationship to the defendant or a prejudice against some aspect of the case.

Even though her daughter was visiting, her conscience would not allow her to fabricate an excuse. She felt strongly that everyone had a responsibility to take a turn when called for jury duty. It would be unfortunate if she had to serve while Cynthia was visiting, but, of course, her daughter had to work anyway. They could still enjoy evenings together.

She got up, straightened the vase one more time, and left the room, smiling at the thought of seeing her daughter soon.

With Alice's help, Jane had finished the bird feeder much more quickly than she had expected. She stood at the kitchen window enjoying the sight of the little feeding station, patterned after a Victorian mansion. She put out some bits of fruit and berries. According to her bird book, that was a way to attract her favorite little bluebirds.

Meanwhile, she was energized by the outdoor project and ready for some kitchen magic. Her most immediate intention was to stock up on cookies before Cynthia and her friend got there. She liked to have a good supply in the freezer, but she had an extra incentive today. A friend had given her a Springerle rolling pin, and she was eager to try it.

She assembled all her ingredients, and then took out the special rolling pin. It was carved all the way around with toy and flower designs, making it possible to press the designs into raw dough without an individual mold for each cookie. The cookies were generally made at Christmas, but Jane saw no reason not to enjoy the delicate anise-flavored treats at any time of the year.

Wendell padded into the kitchen to see what she was doing, but he soon lost interest and wandered off. Jane added anise flavoring and grated lemon rind to the beaten eggs and confectioners' sugar. After blending in the flour, she took part of the light dough and rolled it out on a floured board.

Her first attempt produced sixteen little squares of dough, but the designs weren't quite as sharp as she'd hoped. She cut them apart, put them on a cookie sheet and tried again, this time flouring the Springerle rolling pin more heavily.

She was about to roll again when the front doorbell rang. Quickly rinsing off and drying her hands, she hurried to answer it. The door of Grace Chapel Inn was never locked during the day, as guests were free to come and go as they liked. Friends knew they were welcome to walk in at any time, so the caller might be someone unfamiliar with the bed-and-breakfast.

The young girl on the porch, Jenny Snyder, was a member of the congregation at Grace Chapel.

"Jenny, nice to see you. Come in," she invited.

"I was hoping Miss Howard would be here."

Jenny was one of the ANGELs, the middle-school girls group Alice had founded and still led at Grace Chapel. The girls met weekly for Bible study, projects and outreach to the community.

"I'm sorry. She's out doing some errands, but I don't think she'll be gone long. Would you like to come in and wait for her?"

"I don't want to be a bother."

"No bother. I was just working on some cookies. Afraid I can't offer you one yet. Oddly enough, they have to sit overnight before baking."

"I've never heard of a cookie like that," Jenny said, following Jane into the kitchen.

"They're Springerle, meant to be a Christmas cookie, but I wanted to experiment with my new rolling pin." Jane held it up to show her visitor. "Do help yourself to some lemonade in the fridge. I'll just keep working if you don't mind."

"Thank you."

"Are you ready for school to be out?" Jane asked, knowing that she was resorting to the conversational gambit adults always used with young people.

"Way ready," Jenny said as she stared into the interior of the fridge and took out a pitcher of lemonade. She poured it into a glass Jane provided, then sat at the kitchen table to watch Jane work.

The second try at putting designs on the cookies was much better, and Jane made a mental note to be generous when she floured the Springerle pin. With her attention divided between the dough on the cutting board and her guest, she didn't hear Alice come home until she stepped into the kitchen.

"Jenny, how nice to see you," Alice said.

"Hi, Miss Howard. I brought the sign-up schedule. Everyone but Ashley has picked a time. She's going to her grandmother's for the summer and didn't see any reason to learn how to do the project when she's not going to be here."

"I'm delighted that the rest of you have volunteered," Alice said.

"The ANGELs have a new project?" Jane asked.

"Jenny can tell you as well as I can," Alice said, deferring to her ANGEL.

"We're going to work with young kids at the library. We'll read stories, do crafts, that sort of thing. Until school is over, it will be a small group on Saturday mornings and after school. Miss Komonos wants children to start enjoying the library while they're still little. This summer we'll have different groups for different ages if enough sign up."

"Sounds great," Jane said, separating the individual squares of dough and putting them on a buttered cookie sheet.

"Anyway, here's the schedule," Jenny said, taking an oft-folded sheet of notebook paper from her jeans pocket. "I brought it over so you won't have to worry about not having enough help. Miss Komonos is going to put a notice about the program in the newspaper so we should get plenty of little kids."

"Wonderful!" Alice said, beaming.

"Well, I have to go. I hope your cookies come out well, Ms. Howard." Jenny swallowed the last of her lemonade and politely carried the empty glass to the sink.

"Thank you so much, Jenny."

Alice walked the girl to the front door and came back to the kitchen still smiling.

"Well, that is a relief," she said. "Sometimes it's hard to tell whether the girls are enthusiastic about a project. Judging by this list, we should have a great program at the library."

"I'm sure Nia Komonos will be thrilled. She's done so much to build up interest since she took over as librarian," Jane said.

"Those look like Christmas cookies," Alice said, looking at the second pan Jane had prepared.

"Never too soon to get ready for the holidays," Jane said with a laugh. "Actually, I just wanted to try out my new rolling pin. In addition to these, do you think Cynthia would rather have snickerdoodles or butterscotch brownies?"

"I suspect you're going to bake both and give her a choice."

"The trouble with sisters is that they know each other too well," Jane said with a wink.

Chapter Two

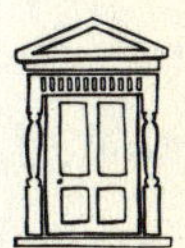

Jane got up early to make breakfast for the traveling couple and for the salesman who had stayed at the inn the night before. Freshly baked corn bread was the perfect complement to one of her specialties, an asparagus omelet. She used sour cream and softened cream cheese in the egg mixture along with some minced onion and seasonings. She folded spears of asparagus inside each omelet and topped the omelets with a small amount of hollandaise sauce.

Since the guests were in a hurry to be on their way, she was able to clear the table and clean up very quickly, allowing her time to write out her shopping list before her sisters came down for breakfast. By the time Louise entered the kitchen, Jane was ready for a morning trip to the supermarket in Potterston where she would need to go to get ingredients for the dinner to welcome Cynthia.

"Good morning. Did you sleep well?" she asked Louise.

"Apparently I slept too long to be of any help."

"Our guests wanted to leave especially early. It worked out well for me because I have a lot to do today."

"You do a lot every day," Louise reminded her. "Cynthia won't expect a banquet. You don't have to work so hard."

"It's not work. You know that I love fixing special meals. What would you like for breakfast?"

"Just bran flakes and juice. I can get them myself. There is something I want to tell you before you leave for the store. I may not be here all the time while Cynthia is visiting."

"Oh?"

"I've been called for jury duty beginning on Monday. I hope I won't be picked for a trial while she's staying with us, but if I am, I'll have to serve."

"Serve?" Alice asked as she walked into kitchen.

"Louise has been called for jury duty beginning Monday."

"Only if they pick me. They call more than they need every time. Maybe I'll be lucky and be dismissed. I understand quite a few cases are settled out of court at the last minute. That could happen to the one scheduled to begin Monday," Louise said.

"That's always a possibility, I suppose," Jane said.

"I wouldn't mind having my turn as a juror postponed. My students are working hard for their spring piano recital, so this is a bad time to be gone even if Cynthia weren't coming."

"I don't imagine jury duty is ever really convenient for anyone," Alice said.

"I didn't intend to complain," Louise was quick to explain. "There's no question about doing it. I just wanted you to know that it's a possibility. If I have to be gone all day for several days, my students will have to be rescheduled. I can still do the inn's bookkeeping at night, but it will make more work around here for the two of you."

"It won't matter. I'm on vacation," Alice assured her.

"What are sisters for?" Jane said nonchalantly.

"You're both dears." Louise smiled. Things had a way of working out well if she relied on her faith and those she loved.

Alice finished sweeping the front porch in midafternoon and glanced at her watch, expecting her niece's arrival at any time. She was delighted that her time off coincided with the visit. She couldn't love her niece more if she were her own daughter.

She was about to go inside when she heard the sound of a car coming down the quiet street in front of the inn. She turned to see Cynthia's blue hatchback pulling into the driveway. Alice hurried to the parking lot to greet her niece.

"Aunt Alice! How wonderful to see you." Cynthia walked around the front of the auto and hugged her aunt.

"It's been too long," Alice said. "You look so stylish. What happened to the little girl who would wear anything as long as it was yellow?"

Alice looked with admiration at Cynthia's pantsuit with textured dark brown-on-brown stripes woven into the cloth. It had a modern shape with slender-legged trousers and a fitted jacket with a notched collar and fabric belt. Cynthia wore it with a silky white mock turtleneck and brown leather pumps with small stacked heels. The suit complemented her tall, slim build and sleekly cut long, dark brown hair, legacies from her father. Her sparkling blue eyes were like her mother's.

"I had to stop at the office on my way out of town," Cynthia said to explain her fashionable outfit. "Joanna needed to pick up some work to bring here."

She nodded at a young woman who was hanging back by the open passenger door.

"Aunt Alice, this is Joanna Gordon. Joanna, my aunt, Alice Howard."

"I'm so pleased to meet you, Miss Howard."

The young woman who stepped forward and offered her hand was thinner and shorter than Cynthia. Her long, reddish-blond hair looked wispy and untrimmed. Her complexion was startlingly pale with a light brushing of freckles. She was wearing a long green print skirt with black rubber flip-flops and a sleeveless black top that further washed out her coloring and emphasized her unusually thin arms. She was slightly stoop-shouldered and moved languidly.

"We're very happy to have you, Joanna. Do call me Alice."

"It's so kind of you to let me stay. I'll try not to be a bother. I have so much work to do while I'm here that you'll hardly know I'm around."

"Joanna is editing her first book on her own," Cynthia explained.

"It's in the beginning readers' line, first to third grades," Joanna said. "In the story twins visit their great-aunt and discover a little elf in her garden. Of course, the aunt doesn't believe them."

"You can tell Aunt Alice more about the book later," Cynthia said with a slight hint of impatience. "Let's get our things out of the car and go inside."

It was totally unlike Cynthia to be cross with anyone. Maybe Louise was right, Alice thought. Maybe there was something unusual about Joanna's coming with Cynthia. She helped the two women carry their luggage, laptop computers and several canvas bags of books and papers into the inn. Cynthia explained to Joanna how her mother and aunts had come to open a bed-and-breakfast after her minister-grandfather had passed away.

"This old house was just too big as a residence. Taking in guests was a wonderful compromise," Cynthia said with pride in their accomplishments. "Aunt Jane could be cooking in a top restaurant, so you're in for culinary delights while you're here."

Cynthia's commentary was warm and welcoming. Alice decided that she was imagining tension where it didn't exist. After all, her niece must be tired after hours of driving.

By the time they'd brought the various bags and satchels to the foot of the stairs, Louise heard them and came out from the parlor, enthusiastically hugging her daughter and warmly welcoming Joanna. Jane heard the commotion and came downstairs, smiling broadly at the visitors.

"This is my other aunt, Jane," Cynthia enthused.

"I'm so pleased—oh no!" Joanna made a sound that was somewhere between a shriek and a howl.

"What's wrong?" Cynthia asked in a calm voice, seemingly the only one who hadn't been startled by the outburst.

"The cat. It mustn't touch me. I'll get terrible hives if it rubs against me."

"Oh, we'll keep Wendell from doing that," Jane said, scooping him up and holding him.

"You don't understand. Cats know. As soon as no one is looking, he'll do that feline thing and slither up to me. If a cat even touches me, I get horrible red bumps."

"You're allergic to cats?" Cynthia asked.

"Just if they touch me. Can you put it somewhere? The itching really drives me crazy when I get hives."

"Of course, we'll take care of it," Alice assured her. "For now, I'll put him in the pantry. I'm a nurse. I understand how devastating an allergy can be."

"Oh, thank you. I am so sorry to be a bother when I've only just been here a few minutes."

"It's no trouble," Louise assured her. "We've had guests with allergies before."

"Do you take medication?" Alice asked.

"I have some," Joanna said. "I packed it in my toiletry bag, but I was in such a rush, packing and stopping my mail and getting all my work together. I'm afraid I left it behind."

"Don't worry. It's just a short walk to the drugstore. They'll have everything you need for the visit, and no doubt we can find some good over-the-counter medication. In fact, there's plenty of time before dinner, isn't there, Jane? I'll go with you to show you the way."

"I would appreciate that so much, Alicia. I need a toothbrush and toothpaste and—do they have a wide range of skin creams? I have dry skin. Nothing helps but one special brand."

"Alice. Her name is Alice," Cynthia said.

"Oh, it doesn't matter," Alice said to make their guest more comfortable, although she'd never thought of her name as a hard one to remember. "Why don't we show you your room. Once you've had a chance to unpack, we'll go to the drugstore. It's fairly well stocked, so you might indeed find your special skin cream."

"That's so sweet of you. But I really don't need to unpack. I'll live out of my suitcases. Wrinkles don't bother me a bit. I mean, I'll just have to repack when it's time to go, so I might as well save two steps, don't you think?"

"Well, there's a nice big closet with hangers if you change your mind," Jane said, still cuddling Wendell.

Louise led the way up the stairs while Alice remained behind with Jane, still a bit befuddled by Cynthia's colleague.

"I suppose I could unpack for her, but she might not like me going through her things," Alice mused.

"She's a grown-up," Jane said in a practical voice. "If she wants to be wrinkled, it's her choice. I hope she doesn't have a lot of food allergies. I would hate to have her get a reaction to my cooking."

"Maybe it's just cats," Alice said optimistically. "It's going to be hard keeping Wendell out of her way. I hate to keep him locked in the pantry the whole time she's here."

"I suppose we could ask Viola to take him. She would hardly notice one more cat."

"That's a great idea. I'll call her. She should still be at the bookstore."

"Invite her to dinner," Jane urged. "I'll have more than enough."

Alice went to call their friend, while Jane confined Wendell in the pantry. He was very much the lord of the manor, usually roaming free over his domain. He was sure to sulk when his freedom was curtailed, but they couldn't let Joanna suffer from hives.

Viola Reed was a long-time friend and Acorn Hill's champion of reading. She owned Nine Lives Bookstore and tried hard to promote classical literature, but Alice could depend on her to order the latest cozy mysteries, her own favorite fiction. More importantly at the moment, she was an avid cat lover. Wendell would be right at home with her feline tribe if Viola agreed to take him while Joanna was visiting.

"We have a bit of a problem," Alice explained after exchanging pleasantries on the phone. "My niece brought a friend to visit, and apparently cats give her hives."

"Say no more," Viola said. "Wendell can stay with me while she's here. Would you like me to pick him up on my way home?"

"That would be wonderful. Also we'd like to have you stay for dinner. Jane is going all out, I suspect, although she's been close-mouthed about the menu."

"I would be delighted," Viola agreed.

Louise left Joanna in the Symphony Room and followed her daughter into the Sunrise Room, eager to have a few minutes alone with her.

"Tell me everything you've been doing," Louise said. "May I help you unpack?"

"No, thank you, Mother. Just sit and keep me company."

"Tell me, what is this project you mentioned on the phone?"

"It's a book for middle-school readers, a fantasy but geared to present-day concerns. The author has written some short stories, but this is her first full-length novel. She has a great deal of natural talent but still has a lot to learn. It's going to be a difficult edit but well worth it, I think."

"And Joanna is working on something else?"

"Yes," her daughter said with a sigh. "She's on her own for the first time, and I'm afraid it's a make-or-break assignment. If she doesn't do well, she may be out of a job. I brought her with me to give her a quiet place to focus on the task at hand, but I'm not optimistic."

"It's going to be quiet in the inn while you're here. She should be able to work without distractions."

"Joanna is her own distraction. She writes poetry, some of it quite lovely, but she spends a lot more time reading and scribbling bits of verse than she does doing her job. I worry more about her work assignments than she does. I hope she isn't too much trouble for you. I know she's not an ideal guest, but I wanted her to have this one last chance to succeed in her job."

"That's really kind of you, just what I would expect," Louise said, smiling with pride.

"Oh, I really like her. She's sweet and has a wonderful disposition. She'd do anything for you—if she remembered. I just haven't felt very kindly toward her today. We had to make a trip downtown to pick up things she'd forgotten, which got the day off to a bad start, because we got caught in traffic. I can't believe she didn't even remember her toothbrush, not to mention her allergy medicine. Sorry, Mother, I don't mean to rant, but the girl is twenty-seven, and I feel as though I'm her babysitter."

"Oh, I think Alice has taken Joanna under her wing already. You can concentrate on getting your own work done, and then we can do some things together. I've been called for jury duty, but perhaps I won't be chosen for a trial while you're here."

"That would be great. I'm looking forward to spending time with you."

"I'm so glad you can stay longer than usual even if you are working," Louise said with a broad smile. "I'm sure Joanna will fit in fine and get lots of work done."

"I certainly hope so—for her sake."

Alice glanced at her watch, wondering if Joanna had misunderstood her offer to walk to the drugstore before dinner. She wasn't exactly pacing the foyer, but she did focus on little jobs that kept her within sight of the stairs. There was no way their guest could have left without being seen.

She'd just about given up when Joanna came down the stairs, apologetic.

"I'm so sorry about the time. I was unpacking some of my books of poetry, and I can never resist rereading some of my favorites."

"We will have to hurry," Alice urged. "The store is only open another twenty minutes or so. Fortunately it's a short walk."

"Oh, it closes this early?" Joanna seemed rather astonished.

"We're a small town. Most businesses close by dinner time."

"I never thought of that. I was mulling over one of my favorite poems. It's by Emily Dickinson:

I never saw a moor,
I never saw the sea;
Yet know I how the heather looks,
And what a wave must be.

I never spoke with God,
Nor visited in heaven;
Yet certain am I of the spot
As if the chart were given.

"The way she expresses herself makes me feel a special glow."

Alice said, "I remember that poem from high school English. It's a lovely expression of faith, and you recited it very nicely. But we must leave now if we're going to get your supplies for the night."

They left the inn, and Alice set the pace, hurrying down Chapel Road toward the pharmacy. She was surprised that she had to slow down several times so the young woman could keep up, but then, the flip-flops Joanna was wearing weren't suitable for walking.

"Here we are," she said, noting on her wristwatch that they had only twelve minutes to make their purchases.

Alice recognized the clerk by sight, although she'd been

working in the store for just a few weeks. Alice would have liked to get better acquainted with her, but this wasn't the time. It wouldn't be fair to expect her to stay late just to chat.

"Now, what exactly do you need besides an allergy medicine?" Alice asked as Joanna started examining a lipstick display on the side wall.

"Do you think coral or dusty rose suits me better?" she asked. "I always have a terrible time deciding. They should have a chart of skin tones and the colors that go best."

"Maybe," Alice suggested tactfully, "you should only get the absolute essentials now and come back tomorrow when there's more time to consider your choices. The store will be closing in a few minutes."

"Oh, of course. I didn't mean to be one of those pokey people who keeps others from going home. I tried working as a waitress once, and some nights it seemed that I'd never get to leave. You can't imagine how inconsiderate some people are."

"The allergy medicines are over here," Alice said. "Do you have any brand in mind?"

"I always use a prescription inhaler. I really don't know what could take its place."

"Maybe you can e-mail your doctor tomorrow and ask him to arrange for a prescription to be filled here. Meanwhile, there are several good choices."

Joanna read the labels on several packages, a practice Alice couldn't fault, but she noticed that now they were the only customers in the store.

"I'll get a toothbrush and toothpaste while you decide. Do you have any preferences about them?"

"Oh, anything. I'm not fussy. And I'll need deodorant, talcum powder, lip ice, body lotion and a really good skin cream. My complexion is so fair that I need all the help I can get."

Alice scurried around trying to find everything Joanna mentioned.

At last they had Joanna's basic supplies piled on the counter.

"Is there anything else?" the pleasant clerk asked.

Alice read her name on the pocket of the green cotton jacket she was wearing. "No, thank you, Gail."

"Oh dear!" Joanna said with distress as she looked at Alice's selections. "I could never bring myself to use blue toothpaste. It always seems like there's something unnatural about putting that color in my mouth. Would you mind terribly if I switch?"

"No, go right ahead," Gail said.

Joanna moved at her languid pace toward the toothpaste display, substituting another for the one Alice had picked.

"That's it then?" Gail asked politely before she started totaling up the purchases.

"Let me think," Joanna said, taking the woman's comment literally.

"That will be all for now," Alice said. "We can always come back tomorrow."

When they were ready to leave, Alice apologized for causing the clerk to work overtime.

Joanna walked at a snail's pace and talked about Emily

Dickinson all the way back to the inn. Alice admired the way the young woman could quote from Dickinson's poems, but she was concerned that the poetry recitations were slowing their progress. She hoped that Jane wasn't yet ready to serve dinner.

While Jane cooked, Louise located the pet carrier that they used to take Wendell to the vet. Getting him into it was sometimes a struggle. Fortunately she didn't have to hunt for him. That cat knew every possible place to hide in the spacious Victorian house.

It occurred to her that Wendell was no lightweight, and Viola usually walked to work. She couldn't expect her to carry him inside his carrier plus his water dish, food, treats, and toys. She made a quick call to the bookstore, catching Viola just as she was ready to lock up.

"I thought maybe I should come by for you in the car. That way we can drop Wendell off before dinner," Louise offered. "I'd like to get him out of the house before our allergic guest comes back from the pharmacy."

"That would be fine."

Viola was waiting outside Nine Lives when Louise pulled up in her vintage white Cadillac. Wendell was none too happy in his carrier, but the grocery bag beside it was well stocked with treats to soothe him. Fortunately he'd been a guest of Viola's on other occasions and seemed to thrive in the feline paradise she'd created in her home.

The first time Wendell had gone to Viola's house, there was some doubt about whether or not he could get along with her oldest cat Ahab, a sleek, gray male with a crooked hind leg. But they'd reached an accommodation by ignoring each other, and Louise wasn't worried about leaving Wendell.

Viola was dressed for work in neatly creased navy slacks, a chartreuse tunic with big splashy white flowers and an artfully arranged white-and-gold silk scarf. Her bifocals made her look even more shortsighted than she was, and her steel-gray hair was like a cap on her head. She waved in welcome, but instead of getting into the car beside Louise, she ducked into the back.

"I'll just get Wendell used to the idea of staying with me," she said enthusiastically, making soothing noises to the cat.

"Thank you so much for taking him. We had no idea Cynthia's colleague was allergic to cats."

"I'm delighted to have him visit. Gatsby will be glad to see you," she said to Wendell.

"Gatsby is your orange marmalade cat?" Louise asked, never quite able to remember all the names of Viola's family of felines.

"No, that's Harry. Gatsby is the big black and white, seventeen pounds the last time I took him to the vet. What surprise is Jane cooking up for dinner?"

"I'm not sure, but it's something Italian. There was a tempting smell of garlic and spice in the air when I left."

"Lovely," Viola said appreciatively. "No one does pasta better than Jane. I'm so happy you included me. It seems ages since I've seen Cynthia. It's always exciting for me to talk with an editor—or anyone who loves books, for that matter."

"She brought a coworker with her. Their offices are being remodeled, so it's become impossible to get work done there. They each brought projects with them."

"All the better. I can hear about both their books."

Chapter Three 

Alice and Joanna returned to the inn just in time to join the others in the parlor. Jane always liked to serve hors d'oeuvres there. Although the room was frequently used for piano lessons, it was a gracious setting to entertain guests. The wallpaper, with its pattern of ivy with pale lavender violets, added to the Victorian ambiance, as did the doll collection displayed on a three-tier nineteenth-century burl walnut table.

Cynthia was playing a Chopin piece while her mother smiled proudly at her daughter's skillful rendition.

"Oh, I never have enough time to practice anymore," Cynthia said, turning away from the keyboard when she saw Joanna. "Did you get everything you need?"

"I thought of several more things on the way home," Joanna said apologetically, "but they'll have to wait until tomorrow. It's so unusual to me, stores that close this early."

"Small-town life," Louise said with a smile. "But it does have its advantages. Viola, this is Cynthia's coworker, Joanna Gordon."

"It's a pleasure to meet you. I'm Viola Reed. I'll look forward to having you visit my bookstore, Nine Lives. I stock a variety of titles, but British classics are my special love."

"How wonderful! I'm always looking for works by the romantic poets, especially Keats and Shelley. I absolutely love Wordsworth, too, and I collect Lord Byron. His real name was George Gordon, although I can't claim any relationship."

"We were just going to have some hors d'oeuvres," Cynthia said. "Please start us off, Viola."

"We'll have to have a long talk while you're here, Joanna," Viola said, turning her attention to the tray Jane had placed on a small serving table that also held a stack of little china plates.

On a hand-painted white, gold and blue platter, Jane had arranged thin slices of toasted baguette brushed with extra virgin olive oil and topped with a mixture of spices and chopped fresh tomatoes and basil.

"It's bruschetta," Jane said, coming into the room with a stack of napkins. "We're having an Italian dinner, so I didn't want the appetizers to be too rich."

"Delicious!" Viola enthused.

Joanna smiled and shook her head when Alice passed the platter to her.

Jane had outdone herself in decorating the table. She had covered the long mahogany dining table with their best cream-colored linen tablecloth and had arranged a centerpiece of daffodils and blue iris mixed with delicate greenery. Whimsically, she had added a tiny bird with real yellow feathers on a thin green stick. The little bird seemed to hover over the flowers. The arrangement was complemented by two large, iris-blue pillar candles.

While the rest of them had enjoyed their appetizer, Jane had put individual Caesar salads on the gold chargers at each place. Baskets of hot Italian bread were placed near both ends of the table.

Louise said a blessing before they began eating, giving heartfelt thanks for the gathering of family and friends.

It was soon apparent that Alice had, indeed, taken Joanna under her wing. She made sure the younger woman was included in the conversation, especially since Joanna had a tendency to keep her head down and not participate.

Louise loved Jane's Caesar salad, even though she wasn't fond of anchovies in any other dish. Jane had a special recipe for the dressing that made her salads particularly tasty.

Louise happened to glance at Joanna's salad plate and had a surprise. As far as Louise could tell, the woman hadn't tasted any of it.

"Would you like some plain lettuce?" she quietly asked their guest.

"Oh, no thank you," she replied. "I'm not a big salad fan."

Jane got up to clear the salad plates, and Louise began helping her, making sure to carry Joanna's. Jane wasn't sensitive, but she would be sorry about serving something Joanna disliked.

The main course was a new recipe, one Jane had adapted from a cookbook, adding her own special touches and renaming it Angel Hair Napoli. Because the delicate pasta only had to cook for a minute or so, Jane couldn't complete the preparations ahead of time. Before she went to the kitchen to finish the entree, she served tiny cups of unsweetened apricot sorbet to the others. As a professional chef, she believed that the small portion of sorbet cleared the palate for the next course.

Louise noticed that Joanna ate most of the sorbet. Perhaps that was how she stayed so slender, by being picky about what she ate.

Louise cleared away the sorbet cups and offered to help in the kitchen. The pasta was done, and Jane had combined it with her garlicky tomato sauce. She scooped out generous servings on the plates, added a spinach mixture simmering on the stove, and topped that with a blend of three kinds of grated cheese, fresh basil, chopped walnuts and seasonings. Her sister admired the culinary masterpieces, then helped carry them into the dining room.

"Aunt Jane, you've outdone yourself," Cynthia said enthusiastically, her voice joined by praise from Viola and her aunts.

While everyone else began eating, Louise glanced at Joanna, who was sitting to her left.

She was pushing the pasta around on her plate.

"Are you all right?" Louise asked softly, afraid that the girl was feeling ill.

"I can't eat this," Joanna said in a strangled whisper.

"You don't have to," Louise said, puzzled by the panic in her voice. "Not everyone likes Italian."

"It's not about liking." Her voice went up in pitch, attracting the attention of everyone at the table. "I'll be desperately sick if I eat even a tiny bite."

"Oh dear, it's my fault," Cynthia said with obvious distress. "I totally forgot about Joanna's food allergy. I should have told you ahead of time, Aunt Jane."

"Garlic," Joanna said apologetically. "I can't tolerate even the tiniest bit. I'm so sorry I didn't think to mention it."

"I had an elderly patient with the same problem," Alice said. "She got a reaction similar to food poisoning if she accidentally ingested some."

"I've never heard of that problem," Louise said.

"It's fairly rare, but it's a serious situation for those who have to avoid garlic," Alice said.

"You have no idea how tired I am of vampire jokes," Joanna said with a faint smile.

"Garlic is used as an ingredient in so many things," Jane said sympathetically. "It must be very difficult to avoid it."

"It's a challenge," Joanna admitted. "Condiments are loaded with it, even some brands of ketchup and mustard. Most salad dressings, canned soups and TV dinners contain garlic. I never do my grocery shopping without reading labels. Sometimes even familiar brands change their list of ingredients to include it, so I never take anything for granted. Restaurants are hard too. Most ethnic dishes like Chinese and Italian are strictly out of bounds for me. There are even crackers that aren't safe."

"And croutons," Jane said with a sympathetic smile. "Tell you what, for tonight I'll whip up an omelet for you. Then for the rest of your visit, I'll make sure that nothing I make for you has even a trace of garlic."

"Thank you, but I don't want to put you to a lot of trouble. I'm fine for now. I don't want your dinner to get cold."

"A taste of sorbet doesn't constitute a dinner," Jane said, showing that she had observed Joanna's lack of interest in the food. "I'll set my plate in the oven, and it will only take a few minutes to fix an omelet. Do you like cheddar cheese and mushrooms? Be sure to tell me if there's anything else you can't eat."

"I love cheese and mushrooms," Joanna said gratefully. "But I hate causing a fuss. Maybe after this I can just fix little snacks for myself instead of making you cook for me."

"You don't know Aunt Jane yet," Cynthia said, laughing. "By the time you leave Grace Chapel Inn, she will have found or invented enough garlic-free recipes to fill a cookbook."

"I do like a challenge," Jane admitted. "So many of my recipes start with a clove or two of garlic that it will be fun to see how I can eliminate it without sacrificing flavor. I already have an idea or two."

By the time Jane was ready to serve dessert, fresh fruit and imported cheeses, Joanna had eaten every bite of the fluffy omelet. Everyone else agreed that Jane's Angel Hair Napoli was one of her best pasta dishes.

It rarely happened, but Jane didn't have a single guest breakfast to prepare Thursday morning. A businessman had stayed overnight, but he had to be on the road by 6:00 a.m. and didn't want to delay his departure by eating. This gave her time to fix a nice family meal for eight o'clock, an hour they had agreed upon.

Cynthia was the first one to come to the kitchen, which pleased Jane immensely. She'd been hoping for a one-on-one conversation. The two of them chatted while Jane cooked and her niece set the kitchen table.

Jane had decided to make two breakfast quiches, using pie crusts that she had prepared the day before. One was a salmon quiche flavored with dill and minced shallots. She knew it was Cynthia's favorite. The other used the same basic custard mix, but she added mushrooms and onions along with grated Parmesan and Dijon mustard, which she carefully checked for garlic.

"I hope Joanna's allergies don't make too much extra work for you," Cynthia said.

"Not at all," Jane assured her.

"I rather miss having Wendell around. It's like a castle without its king." Cynthia finished pouring freshly squeezed orange juice and asked what else she could do.

"Everything is under control," Jane assured her. "Now tell me what you've been doing for fun. Are you still enjoying Boston?"

"It's a wonderful place to live," Cynthia said. "There's always something to do. Mother would love the concerts. I've tried to persuade her to stay with me for a nice long visit, but she seems to go from project to project here with little spare time."

"I don't know how we would run the inn without her."

"She says the same thing about you," Cynthia said with a knowing chuckle.

"But she's the one who keeps us solvent. Without her financial management—my weak point—we'd be in chaos."

"The three of you have a partnership made in heaven. I hope it's not too much of a nuisance, bringing Joanna with me."

"You're talking to an innkeeper," Jane teased. "What we love most about Grace Chapel Inn is that it brings so many interesting people our way."

"I hope you still feel that way about Joanna after a week or so."

Jane didn't have time to ask the reason for her niece's somewhat ominous tone. Alice and Louise arrived together, and Joanna followed only a minute later loaded down with a heavy canvas bag. She was dressed in a long black jumper worn over a purple T-shirt. Her bright yellow flip-flops slapped against the black-and-white checkerboard tiles on the kitchen floor.

After morning greetings and some talk about the work Cynthia and Joanna had brought with them, Jane said to Joanna, "There's a nice desk in our father's old office. We call it the library now, but it's an excellent place to spread out your work. The overnight guests rarely use it."

"Oh, I work much better if I'm in a busy place," Joanna said, leaning her tote against a cupboard. "I need distractions to keep me focused. When I'm alone and everything is quiet, I'm too tempted to work on my own verse or read my favorite poets."

"Are you sure?" Jane asked.

"The kitchen will be perfect. Please, don't put yourself to any trouble on my account. Right now I'm editing hard copy."

Jane didn't think her kitchen would be a good place to edit a book, but she didn't want to be inhospitable.

When breakfast was over, her sisters and Cynthia offered to help clean up, but Jane sent them to their varied tasks. She enjoyed her quiet time working in the kitchen, although today Joanna had staked a claim on the table even before the dishes were cleared.

"Are you sure you wouldn't be able to work better in a room by yourself?" Jane asked, rather hoping for an affirmative answer.

"Oh no, this is a lovely place to work." She was writing and scratching out words at a busy pace.

Jane resolved not to disturb her with more conversation, since it obviously took quite a bit of concentration to edit a book. She'd just finished loading the dishwasher when Joanna startled her with a melodramatic outburst.

"I can't get this to work!"

"Maybe I am distracting you. I'll finish up here in a moment, then I'll leave you to your own devices."

"Oh no, please stay. I love the background bustle. In fact, I feed on your energy. It's just this poem that keeps going through my head no matter how hard I try to concentrate on work. It won't gel for me."

"Are there poems in the book?" Jane asked to be polite.

"No, this is my poem. I was so enchanted by your centerpiece with the little bird that I've been thinking of lines to express how I feel about it."

"I'm glad you liked it."

"'Is a yellow bird among the daffodils more lovely than tiny wings beating against an azure sky?' You see, I have an idea but the words aren't right yet. I hate it when that happens. That line is absolutely terrible."

Jane didn't know what to say.

"The idea is contrasting a tame bird's beauty enhanced by lovely blossoms with the wild bird that flies free."

"Yes, I figured that out," Jane said a bit dryly. She loved creativity in all its forms, but she did wonder when Joanna was going to start the work that she was paid to do.

Joanna wrote, then scratched out some words, then took out a clean sheet of paper and mumbled some words Jane couldn't make out.

"Before I leave, would you like a cup of tea?" she asked. "I have a nice assortment, almost any flavor you can name."

"Do you have rhubarb? I've always fancied that would make a good tea, so tart and still tasty."

"No, that's one I don't have."

"Then surprise me, please. I've never met a cup of tea that I didn't like."

Jane resisted the temptation to try the nettle tea on her and instead made a cup of vanilla spice.

"I wonder if the poem would be better if I used a cardinal among scarlet blossoms. What's a really big bright red flower?"

"A peony," Jane suggested, setting the cup of hot tea on the table beside the canvas bag.

"My parents have peonies lining their driveway. I'm not sure they're quite the shade I need."

"Where do your parents live?"

"Maine. My father owns a couple of fishing boats."

"Interesting," Jane said. "What does your mother do?"

"She teaches elementary school. And my brother Jock works with Dad. I don't have any of their practical skills."

"I'm sure they must be proud of you, working at a Boston publishing house."

"Mostly I think they're glad I stayed in Boston after I graduated from college. They never knew quite what to make of me at home. I wish I knew the names of more birds. I need something yellow and vulnerable like a canary, only wild."

"I have a bird book you can borrow. It's in the—"

Joanna shrieked as hot tea spread across the table toward her bag and the pile of papers beside it.

Jane reacted quickly, grabbing a towel to soak up the spill. "Did you burn yourself?"

"No, I'm so sorry. I reached for the cup without looking and knocked it over. Oh dear, I hope the manuscript isn't wet. I have it on my computer but I much prefer to work with a print copy."

Joanna hovered over the table as Jane carefully separated the damp pages, laying them on paper towels to dry.

"They'll be stained but readable, I think."

Alice walked into the kitchen as Jane was patting pages to soak up as much tea as possible.

"Is there something I can help with?" she asked.

"No, it's under control. Just a little spilled tea," Jane explained.

"I'm so embarrassed." Joanna was wringing her hands, obviously distressed by the minor accident.

"Don't be," Jane said. "Anyone can have an accident. I'm just glad you didn't get burned."

"Once I knocked a cup of coffee over on my lap. That wasn't pleasant, I can tell you," Joanna said, still sounding contrite.

"I should think not," Alice said. "A person can get quite a burn from hot liquid. We've seen it at the hospital too often, especially with small children." Alice looked at the pages spread over the table. "If you can spare a little time from your work, I thought you might like to go to the pharmacy for the rest of the things you need," Alice said. "It's cool now, but it will get considerably warmer this afternoon. I could also show you more of our town. We might stop by Nine Lives too. Viola is eager to show you her stock of poetry books."

"I'd love that," Joanna said. "If the truth be told, I do my best work at night. There's nothing like a dark night when everyone is sleeping to inspire me. Just give me a minute to run upstairs for my purse."

"No hurry," Alice said to their guest's retreating back.

"I suppose I should wash this bag," Jane said, holding up the damp canvas. "Maybe I can just soak it a bit in the sink and hang it to dry outside."

The sisters exchanged a look that spoke volumes. Joanna was promising to be a handful.

Jane said a silent prayer for patience, then smiled at her sister.

"She's well-meaning, but she does have a hard time focusing," Jane said. "She's so different from Cynthia. I know Louise sometimes wishes that she would take more time for herself and give less to her job."

"That would be the pot calling the kettle black," Alice said with a laugh.

Alice enjoyed showing their picturesque town to newcomers and suggested to Joanna that they see some of the town and go to the bookstore before going to the pharmacy. "That way you can sightsee without carrying your purchases all over town," she said.

"I don't want to put you to a lot of trouble. You could just point me toward Nine Lives," Joanna said.

"It's no trouble. I love a morning walk, and my walking partner, Vera Humbert, won't be available until school is out. She teaches at the middle school."

Joanna followed, a pace behind Alice, with flip-flops slapping on the sidewalk.

"Our church, Grace Chapel, is over there," Alice said as they left the inn, pointing to the white clapboard building with its distinctive belfry. "Our father was the minister there for many years. We grew up in the inn, only then it was a private home. My mother died when Jane was born, so Father had his hands full raising us and leading his congregation."

"It's a pretty church. Is it far to the bookstore?"

"No, it's just around the corner from the pharmacy, but I thought we could make a loop around town so that you can get an idea of how it's laid out."

"Yes, that would be nice," Joanna agreed in a neutral voice.

Alice had forgotten how slowly Cynthia's friend walked. She tried not to get ahead of her, but it was like keeping pace with a toddler.

"People in Acorn Hill like to congregate at the Coffee Shop," she said as they passed it. "And if you like antiques, that shop next door is a wonderful place to browse."

She kept up a running commentary, pointing out the Good

Apple Bakery, where a delicious aroma wafted out to welcome customers, and several small specialty shops. Joanna made appropriate responses but showed little real interest. They turned down Acorn Avenue.

"Should you need to use the library, it's right there," Alice said, pointing down the road. They turned on Berry Lane to complete the loop around the little town.

Joanna had her eyes on the ground as she shuffled along past Town Hall, but she perked up when they got to Nine Lives.

Inside, Viola greeted Joanna warmly and quickly invited her to come into the back room where she kept the stock of antiquarian books that she sold online.

"Dear Alice, I don't mean to ignore you," Viola said. "Won't you come back with us and have a cup of tea while we talk poetry?"

"Thank you, but I think I'll go home. There are quite a few things I want to do while I'm not working. You know how to find the pharmacy and get back to the inn, don't you, Joanna?"

"Yes, and thank you so much for bringing me here."

Back home Alice forgot about Joanna while she cleaned out her dresser drawers and sorted through her closet to weed out clothing for a charity shop in Potterston. Although she generally only worked part-time, nursing plus her inn duties and her work with the ANGELs left her with little free time. It was pleasant to be able to catch up with postponed chores now.

She had just finished organizing the linen closet when Jane called up to her to come for their noon meal.

"Louise and Cynthia went to lunch in Potterston," Jane explained. "It's a nice opportunity for them to have some time alone. I can't find Joanna though. Did she come back with you?"

"No, I left her at Nine Lives, but that was some time ago. Do you suppose she's still talking poetry with Viola?"

"I suppose it's possible, but Viola has customers to take care of. Maybe we should locate her before I put our ham and cheese sandwiches under the broiler."

"I'll give Viola a call to see if she's still there."

Alice phoned the bookshop and ended the call with a puzzled frown.

"Viola said she left an hour and a half ago. That's a long time to spend picking up a few things at the pharmacy. Do you think I should look for her?"

"Why don't you call the pharmacy to see if anyone matching her description is there."

Alice was even more disturbed when she learned that Joanna had purchased a few things and left over an hour before.

"I wonder where could she be." Jane mused with a puzzled expression.

"Maybe I'd better take my car to look for her."

Alice drove her little blue Toyota past the pharmacy, trying to imagine where Joanna might go from there. She hadn't shown an interest in any of the shops in town, so Alice tried to cover all the streets where a person on foot might go in an hour.

Joanna's hair was rather badly in need of a trim, so Alice parked and looked inside Clip 'n' Curl. There was no sign of her there. She drove on, parking near the Coffee Shop. There was no sign of Joanna. She even poked her nose into the antiques shop, since she'd pointed it out on their walk.

The town seemed to have swallowed up Joanna. Alice decided to cover all the main streets one more time. She drove as slowly as possible, checking on both sides for a glimpse of their missing guest. Passing the library for the second time, she caught a glimpse of someone sitting on the grass and leaning against a shade tree on the front lawn. Joanna had her feet outstretched, with a plastic bag from the pharmacy by her side.

Alice got out of her car and hurried up to her.

"I've been looking all over town for you."

"Oh, hi, Alice. I hope I didn't worry you. After I went to the pharmacy, I wanted to check out the library. They have a nice little poetry collection, but most of the books are quite old. I guess people used to read more poetry years ago than they do now. I'm afraid I lost track of time."

"Why are you sitting out here?"

"Just resting up for the walk back to the inn," Joanna said with a soft laugh. "When my head is full of poetry, I like to sit and muse awhile."

"Well, let's go back to the inn. Jane has lunch ready for us."

Dear Lord, Alice silently prayed, *please watch over this childlike person and give me the patience to be as a shepherd to a sheep.*

She smiled to herself. It was going to be interesting to have a poet in residence at Grace Chapel Inn.

Chapter Four

Louise found herself at loose ends Friday morning. Not that she didn't have many things on her to-do list, including working on the inn's books and firming up her lesson plans for the following week. Instead of tackling these chores, she sat in the living room flipping through a magazine, making herself available to Cynthia whenever she took a break from her editing.

Louise knew that her daughter had brought a sizeable load of work with her, so she didn't try to pin her down to any specific time when they could visit. Their lunch the day before had been lovely, and Louise looked forward to more time to catch up.

She wished jury duty were not hanging over her head, but there was nothing she could do about that. If she was picked to serve, she was sure that it would be an interesting experience. She wouldn't have to report to the courthouse very early in the morning, so she could have breakfast with Cynthia.

Louise gave up her vigil in the living room and went into the kitchen, where she saw Jane and Alice in the pantry, scrubbing down the shelves and rearranging the supplies.

"What can I do to help today?" she asked. "If I'm picked for a jury, I won't be able to do much spring housecleaning next week."

"Maybe they won't choose you," Alice said optimistically. "They only need twelve for a jury. They probably call double that number."

"That would be nice, but if I am picked, I hope it's a short trial."

"I seem to remember someone telling me that judges don't work very long hours. Even if you have to serve, you might be dismissed in the early afternoon." Jane finished putting canned goods back on a newly cleaned shelf.

"Yes, I don't think it will be very demanding, timewise. Anyway, Cynthia is busy working during business hours. It's not as if we'd made plans to do things during the day."

"Well, I have a plan, and it's called lunch." Jane lowered her voice. "First I'll have to shoo Joanna away from the kitchen table so I can set it."

"She wasn't there just a moment ago," Louise said, "but all her things were on the table."

Joanna's work was indeed on the table, and she'd also taken over three chairs and a spot on the counter to hold an assortment of books and loose papers.

"It might be easier to eat in the dining room," Alice suggested.

"I guess," Jane said, sounding a bit gloomy. "I don't mean to be territorial, but this isn't the best place for her to work."

She moved two rather battered books of poetry from the space where she kept her cutting board and sprayed a commercial cleaner over the surface.

"I'll put some plates around in the dining room. There will be five of us, won't there?" Alice asked.

"No, Cynthia won't be joining us. She's expecting a call from the managing editor any time now. She said that she'll forage for herself later on," Louise said.

"That won't be a problem. I'm serving a bow-tie pasta salad and a vinaigrette dressing with olive oil and minced onions but no garlic. Cynthia can just get it from the refrigerator when she decides to have lunch."

"I should call Joanna," Alice said when the table was set.

"Do you have any idea where she is?"

"She said something about looking for birds in the trees behind the inn," Jane said. "That was quite some time ago."

"I'll go outside and check."

Alice returned alone a few minutes later.

"Not there?" Louise asked.

"Yes, I found her, but she wanted to run upstairs first. She said to start without her, but I assured her that we aren't in a hurry."

Twenty minutes later the sisters seated themselves in the dining room and asked God's blessing on their meal. There was still no sign of Joanna, and they agreed to start without her.

"Sorry, I didn't forget about lunch," she said breathlessly when she finally came into the room. "I had to ask Cynthia something about work. She was talking to our managing editor, so that worked out well. I got an answer to my question and a few ideas on how to solve a problem with the opening sentence."

"You're still on the first sentence?" Louise asked in surprise.

"Oh, I've read the whole thing umpteen times. I was just stuck on how to fix the opening."

"About working in the kitchen," Jane began tactfully. "We have a folding table that I sometimes set up outside when we're having a picnic. I could put it anywhere you like, and you could leave your things on it for as long as you're here."

"Oh dear, I'm in the way in the kitchen, aren't I? That salad looks wonderful. It doesn't have garlic in it, does it?"

"No, I remembered your allergy. About the folding table, I think it would fit in the sunroom. We only use it in the summer because it's unheated, but it's quite pleasant now."

"It's my favorite quiet place to read when I'm not outside on the front porch," Alice said.

"I work better where there's more hustle and bustle," Joanna said apologetically. "Could I set up in the parlor?"

"I'm afraid that wouldn't work well when I'm giving piano lessons," Louise said. "It would be a distraction to my pupils. Some are still a bit shy about playing for an audience."

"The dining room then?" Joanna asked, looking around at the spacious room.

"We have to keep it cleared to serve breakfast to our guests," Jane said.

"I know. I could work wonderfully well on the front porch. I wouldn't be in anyone's way there, would I?"

The sisters looked at each other, and Jane shrugged.

"If you don't think your papers will blow away, I guess it's okay," she said.

"Wonderful! I can watch the world pass by while I work."

"Not much of the world passes by the inn," Louise said, "but you know what works best for you."

"I won't be interfering with anything you want to do?"

"No, not at all," Louise assured her. "In fact, I may not be here during the day next week."

"Only if you're chosen," Alice reminded her.

"Chosen for what?" Joanna asked.

"Jury duty."

"Oh, how wonderful. I was on a jury once. It was a marvelous experience, but unfortunately it ended in a mistrial."

"The members couldn't agree on a decision?" Louise asked.

"We never had a chance to try. I'm afraid it was my fault, at least partly."

"I don't understand," Louise said.

"It was an accident case. A college student riding his bike ran into another boy in a marked pedestrian crossing. Unfortunately, the walker had some injuries, including losing his four front teeth. The defendant was such a nice person. He felt so guilty that he visited the victim in the hospital and gave him a handheld video game player. He wanted the insurance company to pay up, but of course, they insisted on fighting it."

"If the bike rider admitted to his guilt, why was there a mistrial?" Louise asked.

"I talked to the defendant."

"Talked?" Jane asked.

"We both happened to get into an elevator at the same time. He complained about the insurance company not settling the way they should. When I was with some other jurors later, I mentioned what he'd said, and the bailiff heard. He ran off to tell the judge.

So there was a mistrial. I didn't mean any harm. I just felt sorry for the bike rider because he felt terrible about the accident. The judge really scolded me for talking to him. They can be so strict."

"A fair trial is their responsibility," Louise said.

"Well, at least the lawyers wanted to know how the jury would have voted in case they decided to settle out of court. The judge called us back into the courtroom and asked each of us how we would have decided. Eleven of us wanted to give the injured boy a big settlement, but one crabby woman said that her father didn't get compensation when he lost some fingers ages ago, so she didn't see why anyone should."

"Oh dear," Alice said. "It doesn't sound as though she should have been on the jury if she was against anyone getting compensation."

"There was one funny part. The defense lawyer really didn't have much of a case, but he did this odd little dance in the court room. He was trying to show that the victim got hit because he swerved in the path of the bike. I don't think anyone bought that story."

"Well, you had quite an experience," Louise said. "I certainly will make it a point not to speak to the defendant if I am chosen for jury duty. How many days did your case take?"

"I think it was declared a mistrial on the second afternoon. All that legal stuff seems to take forever. I wrote two poems in my head while the lawyers went over and over every little detail."

"Aren't you supposed to concentrate on what's being said?" Jane asked. "What if you missed an important fact?"

"Oh, believe me. They go over every minute fact again and again. I would hate to be on a really big case. It could take months."

Louise hoped that she wouldn't be involved in a long, complicated case, but she was also concerned about the responsibility of making a decision on guilt or innocence.

The Lord had taught compassion throughout His ministry, administering to the sick, the blind and the lame. He fed the multitudes and cast out demons in the afflicted. She tried in her own humble way to follow His example, but where did compassion end and justice begin? Did compassion for a victim demand retribution or forgiveness? She suddenly felt that she needed time to meditate on the duty of a juror.

"I cut up a fresh pineapple for dessert," Jane said after they'd finished their lunch, "if any of you would like it."

"I'll pass, thank you," Louise said. "There are some things I need to do."

After clearing her place and helping to load the dishwasher, she went up the stairs to her room. Whatever the next week brought, she would do her best with the Lord's help.

Alice helped Joanna set up a table on the front porch, although she did think it looked a bit messy to have her collection of books and papers spread out there. She hoped that the wind wouldn't scatter the manuscript all over the neighborhood.

When Joanna was set, Alice went back into the house, thinking about Louise's jury duty. Her sister was ready to serve if chosen, but Alice did hope that a court case wouldn't keep her from enjoying her daughter's visit. Even more importantly, Alice knew that her sister would take the necessity of passing judgment very seriously. Louise always saw both sides of an issue. If she sympathized with a defendant, it would be hard on her to cast a guilty vote.

She wandered back to the kitchen and found Jane staring into space with an open cookbook in front of her at the table.

"Looking for garlic-free recipes?" Alice asked.

"Just daydreaming," Jane said with a laugh.

"You're entitled. Everyone needs a break from time to time."

"I was just wondering what kind of case Louise might get."

"Maybe she won't be chosen."

"If I were a lawyer trying a case, she's exactly the kind of person I'd want on the jury. She's intelligent, fair-minded and conscientious."

"Yes, but how much can you tell about a potential juror by asking a few questions?"

Jane thought for a moment. "I suspect that attorneys are experts at sizing up people. I predict Louise will be selected."

"I know she won't say anything to discourage being chosen. Her honesty won't let her."

"Well, maybe she'll serve on a trivial case, something that will be over quickly."

"Possibly, or she could be disqualified for some reason. I doubt whether they would pick her for a medical malpractice case since I work at the hospital," Alice said.

"Maybe she'll have to deal with a petty crime like shoplifting, one that only involves probation. That wouldn't be such a hard decision."

"Most of those cases are probably settled out of court. What if she gets a felony case?"

"I guess we'd better not worry about it until it happens," Jane said. "If she's picked, Louise will handle whatever she must with the Lord's help."

Joanna began dropping hints Friday evening.

"My college roommate lives in Philadelphia. She's wanted me to visit for ages now," she said wistfully. "I wonder, is there a bus that goes there from here?"

"I think Aunt Jane has gone there by bus," Cynthia said as the family sat on the front porch, enjoying the gently caressing spring breeze.

"I wonder where the closest bus station is," Joanna continued.

"There's one in Potterston, but I don't know what the schedule is," Alice said. Their guest's questions gave her an idea. "Excuse me, please. I'm going inside to make a phone call."

She smiled to herself as she went into the library and closed the door behind her.

Her special friend, Mark Graves, had been urging her to spend part of her vacation in Philadelphia. They'd been close in college but had parted when their differing lifestyles had conflicted. Now Mark was head veterinarian at the Philadelphia

Zoo, and they had recently renewed their friendship. Their relationship had flourished since Mark had accepted Jesus into his life, removing one of the stumbling blocks that had caused them to go their separate ways years before.

Mark answered on the third ring and sounded delighted when he heard her voice. She could see him in her mind's eye, a tall, handsome man with charcoal hair turning white at the temples and a neatly trimmed beard.

"I wonder if your offer is still open?" she asked.

"To visit? Of course. My sister said she can put you up any time. Susan has a very comfortable guest room and would love to have you. How long can you stay? I'm having a bit of a problem with a baby giraffe, but other than that I should be able to get away from work."

Alice smiled, knowing full well that Mark went from crisis to crisis in his job of caring for a virtual Noah's ark of animals.

"Only for the weekend. Cynthia is here with a coworker, Joanna. Their offices are undergoing renovation, and they've come to Acorn Hill to have a quiet place to work. But Joanna would like to visit a friend in Philadelphia. I thought I could drive her there and see you after I drop her off."

"Sounds great."

They chatted for nearly half an hour, as always finding an endless number of things to share. Alice was smiling when she hung up.

"Well, Joanna," she said when she rejoined the others on the porch. "You've done me a favor."

"I have?"

"I was going to stay in Acorn Hill during my vacation, but you've given me a better idea. I have a friend in Philadelphia too. He's been urging me to visit, and I can't think of a better time to go than this weekend. We can leave early tomorrow morning and come home Sunday evening. That way we'll both have a lovely weekend, and you'll be refreshed to get on with your work on Monday."

"You're a doll!" Joanna impulsively hugged Alice, nearly knocking her off balance.

"Are you sure you want to drive into the city with all that traffic?" Cynthia asked.

"I'll be worried if you're driving home after dark," Louise said.

"Why don't you stay until Monday morning?" Jane suggested. "If you wait until midmorning to leave Philadelphia, you can miss the heavy traffic times."

"I thought Joanna would need to get back to work."

"Oh, don't worry about that. I'll take my manuscript along. Maybe I can work on it in the car."

Alice allowed herself to be persuaded. In fact, she hadn't been looking forward to driving back in the evening, but she wanted to spend all of Sunday with Mark.

After the others went off in different directions—Alice and Joanna to pack for the next morning and Louise and Cynthia to take an evening walk—Jane went into the kitchen. She hated to admit it, even to herself, but she would be relieved to see Joanna off for the weekend. She didn't mind making garlic-free dishes or entertaining an extra person at family meals. She could tolerate Joanna's tendency to spread her things from room to room, unable to keep all her possessions in one place. It was the younger woman's inability to settle down for very long that wore on Jane's nerves. The fledgling editor worked in fits and starts, digging into her work with resolve but finding too many things to distract her. Maybe she did do her best work late at night, because she certainly seemed to accomplish very little during the day.

Jane knew her niece well enough to know that Joanna was wearing on Cynthia's nerves too. She had offered the hospitality of the inn for the express purpose of encouraging Joanna to prepare a manuscript for publication. Jane didn't know all the ins and outs of doing that, but she did know from Cynthia that it involved coordinating with other departments of the publishing house—art, manufacturing, marketing, to name a few. A children's storybook was much more complicated than the simple style suggested.

Jane started taking things out of the refrigerator. Alice wanted to leave at 7:00 a.m., so Jane decided to make the same breakfast for the family that she was preparing for the two couples who were staying the night. She would do most of the prep work before she went to bed. She planned on stuffed eggs with Hollandaise sauce.

First, she boiled the eggs, shelled and halved them, and then carefully removed the hard-cooked yolks. Setting aside the whites, she pushed the yolks through a sieve. She added them to a mixture of sautéed chopped mushrooms, Parmesan cheese, tomato paste, and cream, and then mounded the mixture into the shells formed by the whites. She would warm the eggs in a baking dish the next morning and then top them with warm Hollandaise just before serving.

The guests wanted breakfast at eight o'clock, but Jane had two servings hot and ready to eat when Alice came down at six thirty on Saturday morning. She made sourdough toast and put glasses of fresh-squeezed grapefruit juice on the kitchen table, urging her sister to begin eating as soon as she got there. She set out Joanna's breakfast at the same time, believing that she would be down any minute.

"This is delicious," Alice said. "I don't know what's keeping Joanna. Her breakfast is getting cold, and I emphasized that we would leave by seven."

"I'll go check on her," Jane offered.

She hurried up the stairs, not wanting her sister's day to get off to a bad start because of Joanna's tardiness. Knocking softly so she wouldn't disturb their other guests, Jane didn't get a response.

"Joanna, breakfast is ready," she said in a stage whisper that also went unanswered.

The guest rooms all locked from the inside, but Jane acted on a hunch and turned the handle. Joanna's was unlocked, and she quietly slid the door open.

Whatever she'd expected, it wasn't to see the girl hunched over the desk in her pajamas, so absorbed in what she was doing that she didn't look up when Jane came in.

"Joanna, Alice is having breakfast. She expects to leave by seven."

"Oh, is it that late? I woke up with the most wonderful idea for a poem, all about friendship being like a cocoon that nurtures. Listen to this."

"No, not now," Jane said firmly. "Alice is going to Philadelphia because you wanted to visit a friend. You really must get dressed right this minute. I have breakfast on the table for you."

Jane didn't know she could be so stern, but Joanna had brought out her strict side. Really, it wasn't fair to Alice that Joanna hadn't even begun to get ready to go.

"I'm sorry, but I can be really fast when I need to. I'll be down in two minutes."

"Don't forget your allergy medicine." Jane didn't want her sister's weekend to be spoiled by the necessity of shopping with Joanna again.

"I'm pretty certain it's in my travel bag, but I'll be sure to check."

Forty-five minutes later Jane sighed with relief as Alice's car finally pulled away from the inn. She didn't envy her sister's get-away with Joanna in tow.

Louise always looked forward to Sunday services at Grace Chapel, but today there was a special spring in her step as she walked toward the church with her daughter at her side. Cynthia looked especially attractive in a caramel-colored suit with a flared skirt and a fitted jacket. She appeared every inch a big-city career woman, but this wasn't what made Louise's heart sing with happiness.

As a mother, she couldn't ask for a greater reward than knowing that her child had grown into a devout and caring believer. Like her own faith, Cynthia's was woven into the fabric of her being, reflected in all that she did.

Louise was grateful that she wasn't playing the organ for the service and could sit with her family. A guest organist from a church in Potterston was performing today. As the service began, Louise couldn't help succumbing to one small concern: her upcoming call to jury duty and the responsibilities that serving would entail. She wasn't going to pin her hopes on the possibility of being dismissed. In the hush before the service began, she prayed for the Lord's guidance, however the call to jury duty turned out.

Rev. Kenneth Thompson read the Gospel lesson and paused for a moment of silent prayer before beginning his sermon. His love of the Lord radiated out to the congregation. He preached on a familiar theme, the finding of the lost sheep, and though Louise found no new revelations in his words, when the service concluded, she did feel renewed. She made up her mind that if she was called upon to serve, she would carry out her responsibilities as a juror without self-doubt.

Members of the congregation were milling outside the chapel, chatting and enjoying the fine spring day. Several people stopped to say hello to Cynthia.

They were ready to begin the walk home when a stout woman

in her late sixties headed in their direction.

"Cynthia, it's so nice to have you with us this morning," Florence Simpson said, grasping her hand.

"It's nice to be here."

Florence was wearing a lime-green wide-brimmed hat that matched her watered-silk suit. The hat was piled high with white artificial flowers, and Louise wondered, not for the first time, where she managed to find millinery that coordinated so well with her outfits. It occurred to her that it would be perfect for a June wedding.

"How are you, Mrs. Simpson?" Cynthia asked.

"This is certainly my busy season," Florence said a bit breathlessly. "You know, club luncheons, charity dinners, that sort of thing. I can't believe I've been called for jury duty on top of everything I do for the community. There simply aren't enough hours in the day." She arched her finely plucked and penciled eyebrows in an expression of exasperation.

"I've been called too," Louise said.

"Really? Well, I think that it's good for Acorn Hill to be well represented in the court system. Afraid I have to run now. I promised Ronald that I wouldn't chat after church. He can get testy if I keep him waiting too long. He's going to drive us to Potterston. We're having lunch with the president of the Rotary Club there. He wants our ladies' club to help on a project. So nice to see you, Cynthia."

She hurried off, wobbling a bit on the high heels that she insisted on wearing.

"She's certainly a character," Cynthia said with an amused grin.

"Oh yes," Louise agreed. "But she does do a lot for the church. Her intentions are good, even though she can be a bit wearing. What a coincidence that she's on the jury panel."

Jane rejoined them, and they started the short walk back to the inn.

"Florence has been called for jury duty," Louise told her sister.

"Oh my. What if you're on the same jury? That could be a bit trying," Jane said.

A bit is an understatement, Louise thought. Once Florence made up her mind, there was no swaying her. That could be bad when it came to jury duty.

"I'm not going to touch my work today," Cynthia said. "What would the two of you like to do?"

Louise was quiet as the other two planned the day. She wondered how things would go if both she and Florence were chosen for the same trial. The two of them rarely saw things the same way. It didn't matter if they wanted to sing different hymns or serve different refreshments at a church function. Could they possibly come to the same conclusion about guilt or innocence?

"It's settled then," Cynthia said, linking her arm with her mother's. "Don't you think it's a good idea, Mother?"

Louise smiled and nodded. She hadn't heard a word of their plans. She hoped her listening skills would improve at the courthouse.

Alice put on her favorite beige linen suit and coral silk blouse to spend Sunday with Mark. He picked her up early for church so they could first enjoy breakfast at a family-run restaurant that served homemade pastries and omelets that rivaled Jane's.

"I'm glad you're here on a Sunday," he said, taking her arm as they walked to the entrance of the church after breakfast. "We have a guest preacher with us this month, a wonderful woman from the Philippines. I think you'll enjoy hearing about her experiences with the church in that country."

When the service was over, Alice and Mark took a walk and chatted about the sermon and the preacher, which led to a discussion of Mark's overseas experiences.

"You've been so many places," she said a bit wistfully.

"Yes, my work with the zoo has provided me with a lot of opportunities to travel, but there's no place I'd rather be than right here with you," he said, gently squeezing her hand.

So far their weekend had included an afternoon visit to the Rodin Museum, Saturday evening dinner with four of Mark's friends at a French bistro–style restaurant, followed by a wonderful concert. Now they were headed to the zoo.

"I want you to see our baby giraffe," he said. "Her birth was touch and go for a while. I was afraid we might lose her, but she's doing fine now. She's just so wonderful. I know you'll love her."

They strolled around the zoo with Mark proudly pointing out the large animals he loved.

"She's adorable!" Alice said, staring at the ungainly little creature that hovered near its mother. "Have you named her?"

Mark smiled, digging his hands into the pockets of his blue blazer. "I call her Sweet Alice," he said a bit shyly.

Her eyes suddenly felt misty, and she didn't know when she'd been so happy.

Chapter Five

Louise knew to the minute how long it took to drive from Acorn Hill to Potterston, even in the Monday morning commuter traffic. She trusted her car to perform well on the short trip, and she double-checked her wristwatch to make sure it was accurate. She considered it unthinkable to be late. As a consequence, she arrived nearly half an hour before the appointed time.

It seemed overly eager to go to the third-floor courtroom that early, so she wandered around on the ground floor, studying the venerable old building. She'd had brief errands here before, but this was the first time she'd read the engraved metal plaques on the walls that spoke of the architecture and history of the county courthouse. The courthouse had been built in 1915 in the neoclassical style adapted from early Greek and Roman buildings. The characteristics were a symmetrical shape, tall columns in front that rose to a triangular pediment, and a domed roof.

Another plaque told the historical background of places of judgment. The ancient Greek poet Homer had described circles of polished stones where elders settled disputes. The Magna Carta, forced on King John of England by his barons in 1215 to guarantee their rights, decreed that lawsuits be settled in a fixed place instead of following the royal court.

Louise was awed as she thought of all the efforts that had been made over the centuries to guarantee fair trials. She sat on one of the benches and looked around with appreciation at the polished terrazzo floors and the handsome cast-iron rails flanking the broad stairway. Remembering Joanna's experience talking to a defendant in an elevator, she looked around and saw an elevator discreetly tucked away in a corner, obviously not part of the original design. Most of the people who hurried through the rotunda opted to use the stairway, she noticed.

The central feature of the rotunda was a larger-than-life marble statue representing blind justice with scales in her hands.

People passed by, intent on destinations within the building, but it still wasn't time for Louise to make her way to the courtroom. She wondered if any of the people she observed were there for the same reason as she.

"Louise! I was just thinking of you. We really should have ridden here together. Certainly we should carpool if we're both chosen."

Florence sailed up to where Louise was sitting. She was wearing a stylish burgundy suit and a smart little pillbox hat. Apparently Florence had treated herself to some new millinery for the spring season.

Louise thought Florence's suggestion made sense, although she believed it might be difficult to avoid discussing a case during their commute. She suspected that Florence would find it hard to resist rehashing the deliberations.

"Should we go up now?" Florence asked after Louise agreed to ride-sharing, should the need arise.

"Yes, let's." Louise automatically moved toward the stairs, but Florence quickly protested.

"I think the elevator would be safer. Did you know that falling is the most frequent accident among those of us who are mature?"

Louise was sure that the low risers on the staircase were no threat to her, but she glanced at Florence's high-heeled, open-toed shoes and decided to go along with her suggestion.

"I've been watching old Perry Mason reruns," Florence confided to her as they rode upward. "They're so clever. Perry always traps the guilty party with his ingenious lawyer questions. I wonder if we'll get a murder case."

"I certainly hope not," Louise said fervently. "I can't imagine there are very many of those in our county."

Florence continued talking about Erle Stanley Gardner's famous character as though she hadn't heard Louise's reservations about a homicide trial.

"I don't suppose Perry Mason's tricks would work in real life, of course," Florence did concede. "It gives me shivers to think of being on a jury with a really serious case."

Louise thought that all cases were serious to the people whose lives were affected by them, but she knew Florence too well to try to change her viewpoint.

A bailiff equipped with uniform and badge stopped them at the courtroom door and escorted them to the jury room, where they were to wait until they were summoned. A number of people were milling around a long, polished walnut table, making small talk or staring out the windows. Some, like Florence, were flushed with excitement and perhaps feeling a bit self-important. Others were speculating about what kind of trial they might be part of. A few looked positively glum, and Louise heard some muttered complaints from those who felt their time was too valuable to waste on a jury panel.

"I have to be in Maryland tomorrow," a paunchy man in a pinstripe suit complained to the room in general. "A man has to make a living. Jury duty pays peanuts, you know."

After a short while the bailiff came back, introducing himself as George Otto, and took the roll. He checked off names on a list.

"Doreen Conners," he read for the third time, frowning because one member of the panel wasn't there.

He was just about to leave through a separate door that went directly into the courtroom when a red-faced young woman rushed into the room.

"I'm so sorry. I went to the courtroom, and they sent me here. My babysitter was late. My husband travels in his work, and it's so hard to get a reliable person. I have two babies at home and a first grader. By the time I took her to school..." She shrugged helplessly.

"Humph," Mr. Pinstripe said indignantly. "I suppose they'll let you off."

Florence sat in one of the comfortable leather chairs and gave the complaining man a look of scorn. Fortunately she didn't try to lecture him. Louise would have hated to see dissension before they'd even been chosen to serve.

After a wait of ten minutes or so, Mr. Otto returned and called the names of twelve people, including Louise, who were to follow him into the courtroom. Florence looked devastated when her name wasn't called, but the bailiff explained to those remaining that they would be brought in if any of the first group were dismissed.

The courtroom was less impressive than Louise had expected. The judge's bench was raised a couple of feet above the floor, but it was more a desk than the impressive structure often shown in movies. His area, the jury box and the spectators' seating area were separated by dark wooden railings. Louise wouldn't have wanted to sit on the hard benches allotted to onlookers. The jury chairs were upholstered and comfortable. The carpeting had a dark blue and green pattern, and the walls were beige.

Like the rest of the panel, Louise studied the people in the room. A very thin, stylish court recorder had a little desk for her work, and attorneys for the two sides had tables at the front. Four men were sitting at one, but Louise couldn't guess which one of the four was the defendant. If he required three lawyers to defend him, he must have committed a serious crime. This looked as if it would be a major case.

The bailiff called for everyone to rise when the judge entered. He was a slender man of less than average height. He had dark, thinning hair and a lean face with a sharp nose and jaw. When he spoke, his voice was nicely modulated but not very loud. He thanked the jurors for appearing. Mr. Pinstripe, sitting behind Louise, muttered under his breath, "As if we had a choice."

Judge Anton Findlay got right down to business, laying out ground rules and giving a sketchy idea of the case. It involved a

Philadelphia man charged with embezzling, and the trial had been moved to Potterston because of pretrial publicity that might have been prejudicial to the case. The jurors were sternly admonished to answer all questions put to them to the best of their ability.

Jury selection began. It soon became obvious that there was a pattern to the questions asked by the attorneys. They wanted to know if a potential juror had any previous knowledge of the case or any connection to the defendant.

Other questions attempted to discover whether a person would make a good juror. One man in his eighties was dismissed after he admitted that he had a hard time staying awake after lunch. The tardy mother and two others were also excused, but three more were accepted after giving satisfactory answers.

Louise started to form opinions of her own based on the questioning, and so far she applauded the attorneys' decisions to accept the people they had. When it was Mr. Pinstripe's turn, she had her fingers crossed. She really didn't want to be on a jury with him.

"State your occupation, please," the prosecutor asked.

"Insurance consultant."

He answered several other questions in a reasonable manner, but Louise still had her doubts.

"Is there any reason why you couldn't render an impartial decision in this case?" the defense lawyer asked.

"Well, I know I could, but I believe my company does have a policy with Reddenhurst's Department Store. I would have to check to be certain, of course."

Mr. Pinstripe had found a way to be dismissed. No one financially involved with the defendant's store was eligible to serve.

Eleven of the original twelve called into the courtroom had been interviewed, and Louise's palms were damp in anticipation of her turn. She'd played the piano in front of large audiences without feeling anxious, but there was something about the solemn atmosphere of the courtroom and the no-nonsense attitude of the judge and attorneys that was unnerving.

"Mrs. Smith," the prosecutor, Marlene Gottschek, said, "I understand that you used to live in Philadelphia."

"Yes." She'd learned from the other interviews that they liked brief responses.

"Did you shop at Reddenhurst's when you were a resident there?"

"I may have been in the store once or twice, but generally it was more convenient to go to an outlying shopping area."

Her answers seemed to satisfy both the prosecutor and the team of defense lawyers whose names she remembered by calling them Tom, Dick and Harry for Thomas, Richards and Harrison. She became the seventh juror.

New panel members were ushered in to replace those who had been rejected, and Florence was among them. She gave concise answers without unnecessary explanations, and Louise thought she did very well in presenting herself as a qualified juror. She was the ninth person chosen to serve.

When the jury was complete, Louise was surprised to see that it was nearly noon. She'd been so absorbed in the process that she'd lost all track of time.

One of the perks of jury duty in this locale was a free lunch. All of the jurors dutifully followed the bailiff to a nice restaurant a block from the courthouse where a back room had been reserved for their use. They sat at a group of small tables that had been pushed together to form one long one.

At first there was an awkward silence as they took the measure of their fellow jurors. How much time would they spend together? Was this only the first of many lunches they would share? Would there be arguments and holdouts that would distress or anger some among them?

The only thing Louise could compare to this was meeting bunkmates for the first time at summer camp, knowing you would be constantly in their company whether you liked them or not.

Mr. Otto, the court official who would guide them through this experience, told them to order whatever they liked from the menu.

"I wonder whether their soup is homemade," Florence said, speaking up first.

"The specials of the day are Manhattan clam chowder or cream of mushroom," a young woman with large owl-eye glasses said, reading a note clipped to the menu.

"They make their own soup, and it's usually very good," Mr. Otto said, playing the role of host.

Louise didn't realize how hungry she was until it was time to give her order to a uniformed young waitress who was very quick getting around the table. Undoubtedly the restaurant kept the court's business by giving prompt service, although the hour and a half allotted for lunch seemed more than adequate.

When everyone had ordered, there was another minute of rather strained silence. Even Florence seemed to be at a loss for words.

"Why don't we go around the table and introduce ourselves?" Louise suggested.

"Good idea," Mr. Otto said. "You've met me. As bailiff it's my job to make sure you understand the rules and follow them. You'll be asked not to discuss the case outside of the courtroom. It will be tempting to go home and talk about what you've heard with your spouse or friends, but we ask that you don't. The decision you make should be yours and yours alone, not influenced by what anyone else thinks."

After this businesslike beginning, Louise found it interesting to learn who her fellow jurors were. In addition to Florence and herself, there were seven other women, including a real-estate salesperson, a bank clerk and three who were stay-at-home wives: two older women and a young mother. The men included the owner of a lawn-care service who was obviously worried about a long trial, since, as he explained to the other jurors, he didn't trust his brother-in-law to keep their crews on top of the spring work. There was also an accountant, a man who ran a computer business from his home, a high school chemistry teacher and a retired tool-and-die maker.

Louise couldn't remember all the names, but it was nice to know a bit about everyone. She managed to relax enough to enjoy her luncheon salad.

Florence, who sat on Louise's right, was engrossed in talking with Mrs. Bertha Haywood, a pleasant woman in her midsixties who seemed extremely pleased to be paid for being part of a courtroom drama. After several tries, Louise managed to engage in conversation a rather shy older woman on her left. Her name was Ella Girard, and her main concern seemed to be how late the trial would run.

"My husband likes his supper before five," she said. "He's a custodian at the hospital, and he's real hungry when he finishes his shift."

"Yes, I can understand that. My sister works at the hospital. Sometimes she doesn't even have time for lunch." The hospital connection seemed to make Mrs. Girard more at ease with Louise, and they chatted amiably until the bailiff signaled that it was time to leave for the court.

During lunch people lost their initial reticence. Most were chatting busily by the time the meal was over. The lawn-care man and the home-business person seemed to have found some common ground, and the chemistry teacher was talking about the school system with the young mother. To her credit, Florence played hostess, skillfully including everyone in the conversation, reining in her natural tendency to dominate.

Louise felt that they all seemed to be reasonable people and that there was a good chance that the trial would go smoothly and quickly.

When they got back to the courtroom, the prosecutor made her opening statement, outlining the charges against the defendant, Mr. Edward Reddenhurst. Louise's initial reaction was that the charges were rather complicated. Reddenhurst was charged with embezzling from both the department store his family had founded and a charitable foundation his grandfather had established. The prosecution would have to prove that he was, in fact, stealing, even though both the store and the foundation had his name on them. No doubt the case would be presented in easy stages so that all the jurors could understand.

Mr. Reddenhurst, as Louise now knew, was the oldest man at the defense table. He had a thick mane of sleekly styled silver hair and wore a fawn-colored summer suit tailored to fit him perfectly. So far she'd mostly seen his face in profile, since the jury box was at a right angle to the attorneys' tables, but when he looked directly at the jury, the effect was startling. Once, she suspected, he'd been an extremely handsome man, but now she could only describe his face as ruined. His dark tan emphasized a network of deep creases. His expression of arrogance and entitlement was alienating.

Dear Lord, Louise prayed, *give me the wisdom to decide on the merits of the case, not on his appearance.*

There were only a few spectators in the room, mostly older people who perhaps found court cases a way to while away time, but one woman stood out. Reddenhurst turned to nod at her, and Louise guessed that she was his much younger wife. Her skin was stretched tightly over a lean face with high cheekbones and looked more like porcelain than a human complexion. The black of her hair was so intense it almost seemed blue, and she was dressed in a bright yellow suit that plunged low at the neckline and didn't cover her knees when she sat.

Stop judging by mere appearances, Louise admonished herself.

Ms. Gottschek began explaining what the charges meant. She was a slender young woman, perhaps in her midthirties, with glossy mahogany hair pulled back in a bun. Although her navy suit and sensible low heels made her look efficient, at first she seemed to be a bit young to be trying the case on her own. When she began talking, Louise immediately changed her mind about that.

The heart of the case was that, although Reddenhurst served as chairman of the board for the department store that bore his name, it was now owned by a corporation. He had diverted money from the company to support a lavish lifestyle. He'd also falsified accounts to cover money he'd allegedly siphoned from the family's charitable foundation.

It sounded like outright stealing to Louise, but she cautioned herself to reserve judgment. Certainly Tom, Dick and Harry would make strong arguments to refute the charges, although in their opening statements they only emphasized that the defendant had a right to use the funds in question.

After both sides had made their opening statements, the prosecution called its first witness, an accountant who had audited the department store's books. Although what he said was relevant and important, Louise found it hard to stay alert. Her eyes felt droopy, and she even had to stifle a yawn. Were the other jurors battling after-lunch sleepiness? Was that why judges adjourned early in the day? She made a concerted effort to follow everything the witness said, but with only limited success.

Dick, the tallest and most fashionably dressed of the defense lawyers, tried to cast doubt on the auditor's credentials. Failing to discredit him, he questioned him on some very technical details of his audit. Even with her bookkeeping experience, Louise found the testimony hard to follow.

The prosecutor objected several times and the judge sustained her objections. By the time an hour of cross examination had passed, Louise suspected that the defense was deliberately trying to confuse the jury as a first step to winning acquittal. She wasn't pleased with their tactic.

The jury's relief was plain when the judge adjourned the day's session. It wasn't quite three-thirty, but Louise felt as though she'd done a hard day's work.

She left as quickly as possible, but Florence managed to catch up to her.

"Where did you park?" she asked.

"In the lot across the street. I imagine all the jurors did, since the court validates the parking there."

Louise had intended to use the stairs, but she didn't want to be rude by rushing ahead of Florence.

"Do you want to ride down?" she asked, expecting Florence to scamper over to the elevator. Instead she started down the steps, clinging to the rail and huffing a bit before they reached the ground floor.

When Florence caught her breath at the bottom of the staircase, she asked about ride sharing the next day.

"I thought we could take turns," she said. "I'll be happy to start by picking you up tomorrow morning."

Louise couldn't think of any reason to refuse. Florence was a competent driver and unlikely to be late, but Louise was hoping to get right home at the end of the day. From past experience she knew that Florence frequently had little errands to run.

By noon Jane felt a bit overwhelmed. She was alone in the inn and had to answer the phone, clear the dining room table and clean the kitchen, check out the departing guests and register two new ones. Just to make her busy morning more complicated, a man from the county health department arrived for a surprise inspection of her kitchen.

She watched him go about his duties, seemingly investigating every square inch of the kitchen. The inn passed the visual inspection with flying colors, but she would have to await results of the little samples he took to check for bacteria and such. Even though she faithfully followed all procedures for a safe, hygienic kitchen, it was always a relief to have the periodic inspections finished.

Noon came and went, and Alice still hadn't arrived home. She had specifically said that she wanted to leave for Acorn Hill early in the morning.

"You haven't heard from Aunt Alice, have you?" Cynthia asked, coming into the kitchen to rustle up lunch for herself since she rarely ate more than a little cottage cheese and fruit at noon.

"No, I was just wondering about her."

"I told Joanna that she had to be ready to go on time. She

absolutely has to buckle down and focus on her book today. She's been a bit closemouthed about the project. Usually she keeps me posted on every step of her editing. Of course, this is the first book that's totally her responsibility. Maybe she's enjoying her independence. I just hope she's on the right track with any changes she wants from the author."

Jane made tea, and they talked while Cynthia had her lunch. She was about to go back upstairs to her work when Alice came into the kitchen alone.

"That was a trip," she said, sinking down on a kitchen chair. "I feel as though I've been through a Mixmaster."

"Are you all right?" her niece and sister asked at the same time.

"Oh yes, I'll recover. Is the water for tea still hot?"

"Yes, I'll brew you some," Jane offered. "What kind would you like?"

"Strong. Double bag it."

"Did you have trouble on the road?" Jane asked.

"Not with the car."

"Joanna," Cynthia said knowingly. "She promised me not to pull any shenanigans."

"She's a sweet girl," Alice said, obviously making a conscious effort to sound like her usual self. "It's just that she had so many ideas."

"Uh-oh. What now?" Cynthia asked.

"It wasn't any one thing." Alice took a sip of the strong orange-spice tea Jane had put in front of her. "We agreed that I would pick her up at a coffee shop just a few blocks from her friend's house. Meeting there would help me avoid a lot of traffic, and it was on her friend's way to work."

"She wasn't there on time," Cynthia guessed.

"When she didn't come and didn't come, I called on her cell. She'd forgotten about meeting me there and was waiting at her friend's home. I went to get her, but I got confused in the morning rush hour traffic and ended up going miles out of my way. When I did get to the apartment—"

"Joanna wasn't ready," her niece interrupted. "Then she had to make an urgent stop at some inconvenient place."

"Yes, to get flowers to thank her friend for the hospitality. It was a nice gesture, but we couldn't find a flower shop. I finally found a supermarket with a flower department."

"Then you had to go back to the apartment, but since Joanna didn't have a key, she had to find a neighbor who would keep them until the friend got home from work. Aunt Alice, I'm so sorry. I should have warned you that taking Joanna to Philadelphia might be a disaster."

"Dear, don't feel that way. I'm just tired. I had a wonderful weekend. It was so nice to see Mark, and we went to a lovely concert Saturday evening. And can you believe, he named a baby giraffe after me—Sweet Alice?"

"How lovely. But even after the flower incident, it must have taken you an awfully long time to get home," Jane said. "Did something else happen?"

"Well, yes. Joanna hadn't had breakfast. I didn't mind stopping for a short break, but I hadn't planned on doing it five miles from Philadelphia."

"What problem did she have there?" Cynthia asked with a worried frown.

"Not a problem, really. We saw a sign for an antique shop near where we stopped to eat. She was dying to visit it for a quick look. Trouble was the sign made it seem that it was just off the highway. I must have gone ten miles before I found it. The owners' specialty was old books. Joanna was delighted. I thought she was going to handle every book in the store. At last she found a book of poetry by a Scot named James Macpherson. I'd never heard of him, but she was excited to find his work. He was involved in a scandal because he pretended to find some old Gaelic poems, but actually, he had written them himself. He got rich and went into parliament in Britain, where he was especially opposed to freedom for the American colonies."

"Joanna does know about poets," Cynthia conceded.

"Well, she said Macpherson helped start some movement, romantic, I think. Napoleon took a book of his poems with him to Moscow when he invaded Russia."

"Where he lost his army and saved his own hide," her niece commented.

"Speaking of lost, I got lost finding my way back to the highway," Alice admitted.

"I had reservations about bringing Joanna here," Cynthia admitted. "She has a good heart and always means well, but she doesn't focus effectively on anything except poetry. I thought this was a way to save her job, but now I'm not so sure."

"Well, she is an interesting person," Alice said with a forgiving smile. "Eventually I'll forget about the irritating trip and remember how nice it was that she found a special book."

Chapter Six

When Louise got home from her first day at court, she suddenly realized that she had forgotten to cancel her lessons. There was only time to rush into the kitchen for a glass of lemonade before her first pupil was scheduled to arrive.

"How did it go?" Jane asked, looking up from the cabbage she was shredding for slaw.

"Oh, well enough, I suppose. I was picked for the jury. I'll have to tell you about it later."

When she got to the parlor, Janet, her student, was already waiting for her lesson, sitting on the piano bench and carefully picking out notes. She was one of the youngest of Louise's pupils, but she'd already demonstrated an excellent attitude.

Louise tried hard to concentrate, but her mind kept wandering back to the courtroom. It wasn't fair to any of her students if she rushed in late and unprepared. Until the trial was over, the only solution was to reschedule all her lessons, even though it meant giving up some evenings and Saturday morning.

The child's mother wasn't pleased about switching times when she came to pick up her daughter, even though she had first choice of alternate dates.

"I have two boys in sports," she explained. "One has scouts, and the other is in confirmation class. Janet has dancing lessons too. My calendar is so crowded I can hardly find space to write more things."

"I understand," Louise said, explaining her dilemma with jury duty.

They agreed to skip the next lesson, and Louise would call when she was able to resume their present schedule.

The next two pupils were more amenable to temporary changes, but Louise was exhausted when the last student left. She had no choice but to call everyone on her list and reschedule or cancel.

She went up to her third-floor bedroom, closed the door and kicked off her shoes. She'd read somewhere about the value of "power naps," basically short sleeps lasting only ten minutes or so. She definitely needed to recharge her batteries after all that had happened that day, so she lay flat on her back on top of the fluffy quilt that covered her bed, sighing deeply and willing her muscles to relax. After a few minutes she felt a sense of well-being steal over her. Then she let her mind wander to the day's events.

Rehashing what she'd seen and heard in the courtroom wasn't conducive to rest. She got up and went into the bathroom to splash cold water on her face, not recommended for skin care at age sixty-five but pleasantly refreshing.

After dinner she intended to call all her remaining pupils and pay some of the inn's bills. Then possibly she could get to bed early. She hoped that a good night's sleep would renew her energy.

"I invited Aunt Ethel for dinner," Jane said when Alice joined her in the kitchen. "She was so disappointed that her garden tour trip coincided with Cynthia's arrival. When I saw her come home this afternoon, I asked if she'd like to join us. I know she's dying to see Cynthia, and no doubt she's curious about Joanna."

"I'm sure she is," Alice said, smiling at the thought of their aunt's curiosity. She loved her father's half-sister but was sometimes amused by her eagerness to know everything that happened at the inn and in the town. Her husband, Bob Buckley, had been a farmer, and they'd raised three children on the farm. When he passed on, she'd happily moved into the renovated carriage house next door to Grace Chapel Inn. After years of relative isolation in the country, she thrived on life in Acorn Hill and had become something of a town character with her flaming henna hair and gregarious ways.

"Louise looked all done-in when she got home," Jane said. "I hope she isn't tied up too long with jury duty."

"Did she say what case she got?"

"No, and we'd better not ask any questions in front of Aunt Ethel," Jane cautioned.

"As if you need to tell me that." Alice laughed.

Cynthia came downstairs before dinner was ready and offered to set the table, but Jane had already done it.

"Aunt Ethel is coming, so I thought we would eat in the dining room. She always appreciates a little formality," she explained.

"Oh, good. I'm eager to see her. Has Mother come home yet?"

"She's home, but I think she's upstairs in her room," Jane said

They were interrupted by the loud click of heels in the foyer. Aunt Ethel often liked to come through the front door for special occasions. She entered the kitchen looking lovely in a dark purple dress that draped attractively over her somewhat plump figure. She was wearing a necklace of silver beads made by Native Americans, a treasured souvenir of a trip to the West that her family had taken when the children were young.

After lovingly greeting her grandniece, Ethel declared, "I could smell Jane's wonderful cooking all the way to the carriage house. I'm so happy you invited me to join you."

"We're pleased to have you," Alice said, rather doubting that the aroma of Jane's stuffed pork chops with fried apples had carried that far. Still, it was a menu designed to please their aunt, who had cooked hearty meals for her farmer-husband throughout their marriage.

"Tell me about the young lady who came with you, Cynthia," Ethel said, fishing for information with good-humored intent.

"She'll be down for dinner, and you can learn all about her, Auntie. What have you been doing to keep busy?"

Ethel was never one to let a question like that go unanswered, and she was still giving details about her Bunco club when Louise came into the kitchen.

"Louise, I was just telling Cynthia that one of my Bunco friends gave me a pot of impatiens. I thought I might plant them in front of my living room window."

"I'll be happy to do it for you," Jane offered.

"Oh, no thank you, dear. A little outdoor activity is good for me."

The family group became so absorbed in catching up that no one noticed Joanna until she spoke.

"I hope I'm not late," she said, even though it was considerably past the time Jane had told her.

"I'm just ready to serve," Jane said. "Please be seated in the dining room."

Ethel, Cynthia and Joanna took their places while Alice, Jane and Louise brought the food to the table. They seated themselves, and Louise asked Alice to lead them in a blessing, although she was usually the one who said a prayer before meals.

"And especially, dear Lord, thank You for the love and fellowship among those assembled here," Alice prayed. "Thank You for blessing us with a loving and supportive family and good friends to share our lives. Amen."

Ethel's presence did indeed prove to be a blessing for the success of the dinner. She immediately began a conversation with Joanna and seemed fascinated by everything the younger woman had to say.

"I scarcely know a sonnet from a limerick," Ethel admitted, "but I do love a pretty poem about flowers and trees and such."

"Some of the greatest poets wrote about their love of nature," Joanna said, encouraging her to remember some verses she liked.

"I like the one about stopping by woods," Ethel said. "My grandfather kept a horse-drawn sled, and riding in it was one of my favorite things in the world when I was a child. 'My little horse must think it queer to stop without a farmhouse near.'"

"That's Robert Frost," Joanna said. "'Stopping by Woods on a Snowy Evening.' I love that poem."

"Remember the ending: 'And miles to go before I sleep'?" Ethel asked. "When I was learning the poem in school, I didn't understand what that had to do with not being ready for death, but now I understand. It seems to talk to me."

"Yes, that's what good poems do." Joanna had seemingly forgotten about eating. "Frost had important thoughts about everything." She turned toward Louise. "He even had something to say about jury duty, or at least there's a saying that's attributed to him: 'A jury consists of twelve persons chosen to decide who has the better lawyer.'"

Everyone laughed, although Louise could see the truth in the statement.

"How do you remember a quote like that?" Ethel asked.

"It's a gift," Joanna said, obviously pleased. "I guess I have a photographic memory when it comes to words. Now if I could just remember what I'm supposed to do tomorrow and the next day."

The others joined in as she laughed at her own absentmindedness, but Alice felt compassion for their young visitor. She was good-hearted and blessed with a gift for poetry, but not terribly adept at life skills. Alice wondered if anyone else had noticed that Joanna was wearing one yellow flip-flop and one black one.

"Did you have a productive day with your editing?" Alice asked, knowing that Cynthia was very concerned because Joanna seemed to be going over and over her manuscript, making changes with every reading. She didn't know how the process worked, but how much did an editor need to alter and refine a children's book?

"I talked to the art editor," Joanna said, "but we're miles apart on the scenes to be illustrated. She wants to retell the whole story in pictures, but I want children to read the words to know what's happening."

Ethel, who sometimes lost the thread of conversations, abruptly changed the subject.

"I'm having my hair cut tomorrow, but I can't decide how short I want it."

"Is there a good beauty salon in town?" Joanna asked. "I've been meaning to have my hair styled for ages."

"Oh yes, we have Clip 'n' Curl. Betty does a lovely job. If you like, I'll ask if she can take you tomorrow. We could go together."

"That would be so kind of you," Joanna said enthusiastically. "I have such wispy hair that it flies all over the place when it gets too long."

Alice noticed that she'd been too busy talking to do justice to her meal, other than to scrape the pork chop stuffing into a little pile next to the fried apples. That girl did have unusual eating habits.

"We have a date then," said Ethel. "I'll call first thing in the morning and leave a message with Jane about whether Betty has time for you. Jane is always up bright and early. I don't know where she gets the energy."

The dinner came to a sweet conclusion with key lime pie for dessert. Joanna excused herself to go work on her manuscript after Jane insisted her help wasn't needed in cleaning up. Alice helped Jane clear the table while Cynthia walked their aunt home to the carriage house. They shooed Louise away from the kitchen, knowing that she had calls to her students to make before going to bed.

"I was dying to ask Louise about the case, but it didn't seem right to be nosy about it," Alice said.

"No, I'm sure that she received some warning about not discussing the case outside the jury room." Jane brushed a stray lock of hair away from her forehead and smiled a bit wearily. "I think that's best. She'll tell us about it when she can."

Alice nodded in agreement.

On Tuesday Jane set herself the goal of replenishing her cookie supply in the freezer. Besides having cookies available to guests as an afternoon treat, she liked to serve them to visitors and to bring them to shut-ins. A supply in the freezer came in handy for meetings and other occasions that came up. To Jane it was much easier to have a baking marathon from time to time than to make just a dozen or two at a time.

As soon as the guests and family had had breakfast, she got started. There were favorites that she always made, chocolate chip and snickerdoodles. She liked to have a supply of sugar-free oatmeal crisps for an elderly diabetic friend and anyone else who might need to restrict carb intake.

Those she would make for sure, but she wanted to try

something new. While she waited for the first batch to bake, she thumbed through a couple of her favorite books for recipes she could use without a trip to the grocery store. Fortunately her pantry was well stocked with the good ingredients that made her cookies special.

Almond macaroons sounded particularly tempting, but unfortunately she didn't have the almond paste necessary to make them. She thought about cornflake macaroons but, delicious as they were, they did not freeze successfully. She didn't have time for cookies that had to be rolled out and cut into shapes, nor did she want to make frosting.

She narrowed the choice down to a chewy chocolate cookie made with both melted unsweetened squares and chips, or spicy pumpkin-raisin cookies. Things were moving along so smoothly this morning that she decided to make both.

One of the things she liked best about cookie making was the wonderful smell that filled her kitchen. No candle or incense could compare to the rich, sweet fragrance of a pan of hot cookies. She had a rack of snickerdoodles cooling on the counter when the aroma attracted her niece.

"Aunt Jane, you're torturing me. I can smell freshly baked cookies in my room," Cynthia said as she came into the kitchen.

"Help yourself," she invited with a pleased smile. "I'll make you a cup of tea if you like."

"I'd love one. Even overworked editors deserve a tea break, don't they?"

"Is your work going well?"

"Very well, thank you. It's amazing how much more I get done here with no one to interrupt me. This place is an oasis of tranquility compared to our offices in Boston. I should be able to clear up a lot of busy work besides finishing the book. There are always so many books in our slush pile."

"Your slush pile?"

"Unsolicited manuscripts. Some are dreadful, of course, but every once in a while we get lucky and find a marvelous new author. It's time-consuming to go through all of the manuscripts that come in, and I'm always much slower at it than I'd like."

"Well, I'm glad you're getting so much done. Maybe by the time your mother is through with jury duty, you can take a day off to spend with her."

"I certainly will if she's done before I have to leave. I only wish Joanna would finish her work. I was counting on her to help read the unsolicited manuscripts, but she doesn't seem satisfied with all the changes she's made. Has she come back from her hair appointment yet?"

"Not that I know."

"Well, how long can it take to get a haircut?"

"Aunt Ethel does like to make a production of it," Jane warned, "but Betty keeps a pretty tight schedule. They're due back any minute."

She made a pot of lemon verbena tea. While it was brewing, Alice came into the kitchen, also lured by the fragrance of Jane's cookies. She joined Cynthia in sampling a snickerdoodle. There were few things that tasted better than a cookie fresh from the oven.

After they all had tea and had indulged in another cookie, Cynthia was about to go back upstairs to work when the front door of the inn opened and closed. Jane recognized her aunt's footsteps and went to greet her.

"Aunt Ethel, how did—"

"I've lost that girl."

Behind her Jane heard Cynthia groan.

"Oh, I'm sure she'll find her own way back here," Jane said in a soothing voice.

"She doesn't know her right foot from her left. Every time we came to a corner, she automatically turned in the wrong direction. I knew I shouldn't have left her alone at the beauty salon."

"She's twenty-seven years old," Cynthia said. "I'm sure she can look after herself."

"You don't understand. I promised to go back to the hair place so we could walk home together. I hurried over to the library to return a book. I didn't even look for another one to take out, but a friend was there. We only chatted a few minutes. I'm sure of that. But when I got back to Clip 'n' Curl, Joanna was gone. Betty said she'd only wanted a trim, so it didn't take long. I don't know why she didn't wait for me. I looked all over for her, but she wasn't anywhere."

"She probably just forgot that you were coming back," Alice said in a soothing voice.

"It's not your fault if she wandered off, Aunt Ethel. You were nice to take her there. I'm sure she'll find her way home. Why don't I fix you a cup of tea, and you can sample one of my freshly baked chocolate chip cookies."

"Oh, thank you, Jane. I do need a little nourishment after practically running back here. But where do you suppose she went?"

"Unless I miss my guess, she headed straight for the bookstore," Alice said. "Books are like a magnet for Joanna. You have your tea, Aunt Ethel, and I'll give Viola a call at Nine Lives."

Alice was right. Viola told her that Joanna was indeed at the bookstore looking through a box of old books that she'd bought at a country auction just last week.

Cynthia shook her head in disappointment. "It's not just that I could use her help," she said. "She's on probation, but she doesn't seem the least concerned that her job is in jeopardy."

"Oh dear, it would be a shame if she lost it. She seems to love words so much. What better job could she have than being an editor?" Alice asked.

Cynthia didn't answer, but her expression clearly indicated that she wasn't convinced that editing was Joanna's forte.

"Well, I'm glad she's all right. And I'd hate for her to lose her job. Still, it was odd that she didn't wait for me."

"I'm sure she didn't mean to distress you by leaving, Aunt Ethel," Alice assured her. "Things seem to slip her mind quite easily."

"Yes, I know old people who are like that." Ethel reached for a second cookie with a little smile meant to exclude herself from the infirmities of advanced age.

Jane smiled. She liked to believe that aging was a state of mind as much as a physical change, and she hoped to have Ethel's zest for life as she grew older.

Louise didn't feel like herself when she woke up Tuesday morning. It took her a few moments to realize why. She wasn't looking forward to the day as she usually did.

Generally she awoke with a head full of plans for what she wanted to accomplish during every precious hour the Lord would give her. Her first instinct was to give thanks in the words of a favorite psalm:

> *"Give thanks to the* Lord, *for he is good.*
> *His love endures forever"* (*Psalm 136:1*).

Louise said the words aloud before leaving her bed, but her lack of enthusiasm followed her as she showered and dressed for the day in a beige linen suit with a sky-blue blouse. It did give her a lift to dress up in a favorite outfit, and she decided to be positive about the day ahead.

She prayed before leaving her room, asking for wisdom and patience in whatever the day brought.

Cynthia and her sisters were having breakfast when she went down to the kitchen. Two guests, a couple from Indianapolis, were lingering over coffee in the dining room, but Jane had turned her attention to her family. Her waffle iron was out on the counter, and she was taking orders, adding pecans to the mix for those who wanted them.

"One waffle or two?" Jane asked after Louise had a chance to say good morning to everyone.

"Just one, please."

Louise wasn't very hungry, but she felt she should eat something so that her stomach didn't grumble in the middle of the morning session.

"Coming up. What time did you say Florence was coming for you? I should have asked her to breakfast."

"She probably wants to make Ronald's meal before she leaves," Louise said. "I'm a little uneasy about this travel arrangement. I'm afraid that Florence will want to talk about the trial all the way over and back."

"That shouldn't be a problem," Alice assured her. "No one can influence Florence's vote once her mind is made up, and I'm sure you won't be swayed by anything she says."

"You're probably right," Louise said. "I hope we're dismissed as early as we were yesterday. The day seems longer when you have to sit still and pay attention."

"I'm sure you'll be a marvelous juror, Mother. I'm working hard to get my work done. That way maybe we can have a couple of days together if you're done with jury duty," her daughter said.

Jane put the golden waffle on a plate, and Louise trickled maple syrup over it. She passed up the crispy bacon sitting on a platter and began eating.

"Good morning, everyone."

Florence's voice was unmistakable as she came into the inn through the front door.

"We're in here, Florence," Jane called out.

Florence was wearing a sage-colored suit with a pleated skirt that swished as she walked. Unlike the modest little hat she'd worn yesterday, she was sporting a confection in lemon yellow and white with swirls of netting and artfully arranged silk flowers. Somehow she'd managed to match the leaves perfectly with her suit.

"Would you like a waffle, Florence?" Jane offered.

"I shouldn't but I only had a tiny bit of breakfast, just some cereal and juice, even though I made scrambled eggs for Ronald. Maybe just a little one. We have time, don't you think, Louise?"

"Plenty of time," she agreed.

While her fellow juror waited for a waffle and questioned Cynthia about life in Boston, Louise had a sudden revelation. Florence's overdressing for a day at the county courthouse was probably a sign that she wasn't feeling entirely secure in this new situation. Among the ten other jurors, there were very likely some who were worried about missing work or neglecting family responsibilities. Others might be confused by complicated laws and the attorneys' interpretations of them. If she could make things a little more pleasant for the others, it might be some small help to them. Sometimes a little kindness went a long way toward improving a situation. She vowed to try to be a source of comfort for the other members of the panel. As she and Florence stood to leave, she thanked the Lord for giving her this insight. Now she felt ready to be a good juror.

Chapter Seven

Tuesday had gone by in a blur for Louise. The testimony was even more detailed and hard to follow than it had been the day before. They had been dismissed later than on Monday, and that meant that she and Florence got caught in rush-hour traffic leaving Potterston. While it was nothing like city traffic, it did make their commute longer.

When Louise arrived home, it was nearly dinnertime. After a relaxing meal with her family and Joanna, Louise felt ready to tackle some paperwork before she went off for an early bedtime.

Today Louise was scheduled to drive Florence to Potterston. They'd reached an agreement on the trip home the day before not to discuss the case while they were riding together. Florence's chatter about people and activities at Grace Chapel actually proved a pleasant distraction for Louise. Like Ethel, Florence had a gift for knowing everything that was happening in Acorn Hill. She knew who was ill and who was recovering. No member of the chapel went into the hospital or planned a vacation or other special event without Florence noticing. It was helpful to know the names of people who might need a visit or some other kindness, like a plate of Jane's cookies.

Jane was busy serving the inn's lone guest in the dining room when Louise went down for breakfast. Alice was in the kitchen. Louise helped herself to a small slice of mushroom and sausage quiche that Jane had left warming in the oven and joined her sister at the table.

"What are your plans today?" Louise asked.

"The nice thing about being on vacation is that I don't have to make plans," Alice said cheerfully. "Do you have any idea when you'll finish with jury duty?"

"I suspect the defendant's three lawyers will need a lot of time to refute all the charges. I have no hope at all of being done this week."

"That's a shame. I know Cynthia would like to spend more time with you, although I get the impression that she's not finishing her work as quickly as she'd hoped. She expected more help from Joanna. I do admire Cynthia's patience. Joanna is a sweet person, but she's no ball of fire when it comes to getting things done." From what she'd seen, Louise had to agree with Alice's comment. Her sister rarely criticized anyone, and she had taken Joanna under her wing. There was no unkindness in her observation, only concern.

"Whenever I see her out on the porch, she's busy writing. I thought she was being quite industrious," Louise said.

"Oh yes, but she wants every word to be perfect. From what I understand, she finishes one day, then starts over again on the same material in her manuscript the next day. It never completely pleases her," Alice said.

"I wonder what the problem is. She certainly loves words, but maybe she's just not the right person to be an editor."

"I've always believed that success in life involves knowing yourself and what you do best," Alice said thoughtfully.

"No one could doubt that you were born to be a nurse," Louise said. "Well, I'd better be on my way. Florence will be nervous if we don't leave well ahead of time. The judge is strict about starting on time. I tell you, Alice, I'm learning so much this week that my head is spinning. I think I'll be very glad to have had this experience—once it's over."

"Well, I hope that will be soon."

Alice walked with her to the car and saw her off.

As expected, Louise and Florence had more than half an hour to wait before they had to report to the jury room.

"We could go for coffee," Florence suggested.

"Oh, I think I'll pass," Louise said.

"I will too. I don't feel comfortable until I'm inside the courthouse. Silly, I suppose. It's just that being a juror is a little intimidating."

Louise never expected to hear Florence admit that she was intimidated by anything, but the situation was daunting. The jurors had to pay close attention to everything that was said and done. Otherwise a guilty man could go free or an innocent one could be convicted. None of the courtroom dramas in books, movies or TV programs showed the role of a juror quite the way it really was.

Surprisingly, they were far from being the first to arrive in the jury room. Nearly half the jurors had congregated early with Mr. Otto watching over them like a proctor at an exam. He didn't say much, but his presence tended to put a damper on conversation.

"I hope the testimony isn't too complicated today," Ella Girard confided to Louise in a low voice. "It was hard to understand what that accountant was talking about yesterday. I never had any bookkeeping in school. I'm not sure I'm qualified to be a juror."

"You'll do fine," Louise assured her. "It's confusing to all of us now, but I'm sure the attorneys will make everything clear."

Ella still looked uncertain, but Louise smiled and changed the subject, asking whether she lived very far from the courthouse.

"Close enough to walk," Ella said. "I never learned to drive, and my husband couldn't take off work to bring me."

"If you ever feel a need for a ride, let me know. You can phone me at Grace Chapel Inn in Acorn Hill."

"Thank you, but I'm used to walking."

Louise tried to be encouraging, but she realized that Ella was a worrier. She fretted because her cat would miss her during the day and agonized over what to wear to court. Today her choice of garb was rather unfortunate. She was wearing a navy wool suit in a style long out of fashion, and it was too warm for the fine spring day. It wasn't flattering to her very pale skin, but it did emphasize her prim and proper attitude.

"We certainly drew a boring case," commented Bertha Haywood, a woman in her early sixties who worked for the county road commissioner. "I thought it would be pleasant to be paid for just listening, but I struggle to stay awake after lunch."

Mr. Otto frowned his disapproval of the jurors' small talk and reminded them that they shouldn't discuss the case until it was time to deliberate.

The last to arrive was Egbert Foster, the man who ran the lawn service. He was short and pugnacious, his white forehead contrasting with the ruddy color of his face. He came in wearing his usual red cap with a bill, but today the bailiff didn't have to remind him to remove it before they filed into the court.

"How much longer is this going on?" he asked Mr. Otto. "I have a business to run."

"That's not for me to say."

"Some job you have, just standing around all day."

Mr. Otto ignored the man's scornful comment. Louise thought Egbert was out of line, taking his ire out on the bailiff, but she tried to smooth things over by asking him whether he did any landscaping. He relaxed as he talked about his work, apparently taking quite a bit of pride in doing a good job for his customers.

It was a relief when the jurors were summoned to take their places in the jury box.

Louise was as eager as the rest to have the defense begin, but they were only in the courtroom for a few minutes before they were ushered back to the jury room.

"What was that all about?" Lee Denison, the retired tool-and-die maker, demanded to know. "I could be home working in my garden."

At lunch the day before he'd told in great detail about the miniature village he was building, complete with a windmill and a waterwheel powered by a little creek that ran through his property. It sounded charming to Louise, and it was obvious Mr. Denison was eager to return to playing Gulliver in his miniature world.

"A dispute between the prosecution and defense," Mr. Otto explained. "Apparently the judge didn't think you needed to hear it."

"They can take as long as they like as far as I'm concerned," Eve Franken said, flipping her long, straight blond hair back from her face. "I love having my mother-in-law take care of my kids. She has always had plenty of advice for me, but I notice she's not so quick to criticize after a few days with my two- and four-year-olds."

"I wish I had someone I could trust running my business," Egbert groused. "All you have to put up with is some criticism. I could lose my customers."

Louise drew his attention from Eve by commiserating with him. Then she changed the subject, asking his opinion of the landscaping around the courthouse. Eve threw Louise a grateful look, and Egbert was delighted to comment on something he knew about. Minutes later they were called back into the courtroom.

In the short time it had taken her to walk outside with Louise, Alice found that Jane had returned to the kitchen and was nearly finished with the cleanup.

"What can I do for you today?" Alice asked.

"I don't expect you to spend your whole vacation working," Jane said emphatically. "You've already caught me up on all the jobs I let slide."

"Jobs you didn't have time to do," Alice corrected her. "I enjoy working around the house."

"Well, today you can enjoy not having to work. I think we made a good decision when we agreed to have a cleaning service come from Potterston to give the inn a real spring cleaning. We just don't have the time to do it ourselves. They should be here any minute."

"Yes, it was an excellent idea. We had such a good year that it doesn't seem like extravagance to have the service. Maybe I'll putter in the garden to keep out of their way."

"If you can find anything to do," Jane said, suggesting that she'd already done all that was necessary.

Alice wandered out to the spacious garden beside the house, enjoying the neatly laid path and newly spaded beds, where flowers would bloom all summer. Not surprisingly, Jane did have everything in good order. Alice bent and pulled out a tiny weed intruding among the rose bushes, but she had to admit there wasn't anything here to occupy her.

A white van with red letters that advertised the cleaning company's services pulled up before she could go back inside. There were five people, three men and two women, dressed in khaki uniforms with a company logo on the shirts. Alice watched with interest as they started unloading equipment, and then followed them through the front door. The oldest of the group, a burly man with arms that strained the fabric of his shirt sleeves, greeted her politely but was obviously too busy putting the others to work to waste time talking.

Jane was in the foyer going over their procedures and receiving assurances that they would finish before any guests checked in for the evening. The only room they weren't going to clean was the kitchen. Jane preferred to handle the food preparation area herself.

Cynthia came downstairs with a heavy canvas bag. Joanna followed, also weighed down by a tote.

"Aunt Alice, we're going to the library to work."

Even as she spoke, one of the workers was leaning a long extension ladder against the outside of the house to reach the upper windows.

Jane retreated to the kitchen, and Alice followed, wondering what her sister would be doing while the house was invaded by cleaners.

"I've been meaning to clean this drawer," she said, taking out the dividers that separated the knives, forks and spoons. "No matter how hard I try to avoid it, little crumbs always find their way into it."

"May I help?" Alice asked.

"There's really not much to do. Why don't you sit and have another cup of tea?"

Alice declined. Maybe this would be a good time to walk. There were several little errands she could do.

The town was quiet on this midweek morning. She walked past Fred's Hardware but couldn't think of any excuse to stop. The same was true of the pharmacy and the general store. She crossed Chapel Road and started to walk past Nine Lives when she thought of a reason to go inside.

The bookstore had a charm that reflected the love Viola put into her business. It occupied a small white building with a red roof that reminded Alice of the fairy tales she'd loved as a child. A bell tinkled as she opened the beveled glass door with the owner's name in gold. The interior was warm and inviting with cocoa-brown carpeting and taupe walls mostly obscured by shelves and portraits of authors such as Dickens, Shakespeare and Twain.

Viola was alone, unpacking a box of books and putting them on shelves labeled with pine signboards to help customers find the categories they wanted.

"Good morning. May I help you with those?" Alice asked.

"Oh, Alice, thank you, but I'd better do this myself. I have my own peculiar way of organizing my stock. Are you looking for anything in particular this morning?"

"No, I just stopped by to make sure Wendell isn't giving you any trouble."

"He's like one of the family." Viola's face crinkled up in a broad smile. "You know, there's no such thing as too many cats for me."

"We really appreciate your keeping him."

"I'm happy to do it. It's so sad that Joanna's allergies keep her from the joy of having a kitty of her own. There are so many in need of good homes, and she's such a kind girl."

"Yes," Alice agreed.

She did like Cynthia's coworker, but she felt that Joanna's trouble completing her work was going to be a source of difficulty for her and for Cynthia. The nurse in her wondered if Joanna could be suffering from an attention disorder, although she seemed perfectly capable of giving full attention to her poetry.

A customer came into the shop, and Viola had to excuse herself. Alice said good-bye and left, not wanting to interfere with Viola's business.

She enjoyed walking, although it was much more pleasant when Vera could join her. She looked forward to the end of the school year, when her friend would be available for the morning outings together that they both enjoyed.

There was one other place she could go. The ANGELs were scheduled to begin helping with the children's program at the library. She was very proud of the way they'd organized their participation, but she really should stop by and confirm that everything was ready.

For nearly fifty years Miss Gladys Raylor had presided over the library, gently guiding generations of readers to the best the library had to offer. Alice had adored her as a child, and when she passed away, it had been like losing a member of the family. Stepping inside the quiet building, she remembered the lovely face of the elderly librarian, not a conventionally beautiful visage but one molded by kindness. She'd loved blue and had often worn it, a perfect complement to the halo of soft white hair that framed her face in later years.

Nia Komonos, the new librarian, had faced the challenge of replacing a much-loved predecessor with zest and intelligence. Her naturally outgoing nature and pleasant disposition had won the hearts of the townspeople, and she'd brought modern techniques of library science to Acorn Hill in such a low-key way that she encountered no resistance from even the most conservative citizens.

Alice saw Nia standing by the checkout desk, a tall, slender woman with thick, glossy dark hair, a gift from her Greek ancestors, artfully arranged in a bun. She was wearing a pale fawn suit with a high-necked peach top.

Cynthia was sitting at a table in the reading area surrounded by stacks of paper. Alice waved at her when she looked up but didn't go over for fear of distracting her from her work. Joanna's tote was on a separate table, but she was nowhere in sight.

"Good morning, Alice," Nia said, speaking in a muted voice. "I've wanted to talk to you. Unfortunately, I'm here alone this morning, so I can't invite you to come to my office."

"That's quite all right. I only wanted to be sure you're happy with the plans my ANGELs have made."

"I'm delighted. Jenny has been here several times to discuss them. She and her friends have put a lot of work into the schedule and the craft plans. The children will be making some nice little souvenirs of the books we're reading to them. The girls are a credit to you."

"They deserve all the credit themselves. We're all set to begin then?"

"Oh yes, and I've had quite a few parents register their children. If all goes well, we'll continue at least through July. I've wanted to offer a program that will introduce young people to all that the library has to offer."

Alice talked with Nia for several minutes, then glanced over at Cynthia. She was so absorbed in her work that Alice left without talking to her. Joanna was still out of sight, perhaps doing research in the stacks.

After she left the library, Alice walked for another half hour, following Village Road beyond the outskirts of town until she felt that she'd had enough exercise for one day. She strolled back to the inn at a more leisurely pace and found the cleaning van still parked in front. She didn't want to be in the way, but she wasn't quite sure where to go.

She sat on her favorite chair on the front porch, noticing that the table Joanna had used briefly was still set up there. The young woman had wanted a busy place to work, but the road in front of the inn was anything but bustling. In fact, now that Alice was temporarily at loose ends herself, she could understand how someone used to the fast tempo of life in Boston might find Acorn Hill much too slow-paced.

Alice knew that she did her best work when the pressure was on. The busier she was, the more she enjoyed giving her all. She'd always had family, her father and now her sisters, to use as a sounding board for the day's activities. Joanna was a fish out of water in Acorn Hill. Their guest needed some incentive to use her time more wisely, some activity that would encourage her to get through work to allow time for play.

The more Alice thought about it, the more she was convinced that the library program was just the thing to give Joanna a feeling of accomplishment. She was sure Nia would welcome another adult to help.

Alice went into the inn, sidestepping a tangle of cords in the foyer, and found a relatively quiet spot in the office to use the phone.

As expected, Nia was enthusiastic. She welcomed the prospect of Joanna's participation.

Now all Alice had to do was decide how to approach Joanna with her idea.

As much as Jane loved to see the inn sparkling clean, she was impatient to have the cleaning crew leave. They invaded every nook and cranny of the large Victorian house in their quest for cleanliness, and she much preferred to be in charge of her own domain.

Still, she had to admit it had been a good idea to have a commercial firm handle the spring housecleaning. Louise had first suggested it, wanting to reduce the volume of work that fell on all of them.

Jane walked through the downstairs rooms, finished except for the buffing of the floor in the foyer. Crackly white paper provided paths across the newly shampooed rugs, protecting them until they dried. Her sandals had left damp footprints on the paper in the parlor, so she didn't enter the other rooms.

Even though Jane didn't enjoy the bustle of having so many workers in the house, she did appreciate the aroma left by a thorough cleaning: a blend of lemon oil, window cleaner, damp rugs and floor wax. She had selected the company in part because it used environmentally friendly cleaning products. As much as possible, she tried to keep the inn "green." The windows were open to help wet wool dry, and when the crew left, she would light candles to further freshen the air. For now, though, the smell represented a spotlessly clean inn.

The cleaning crew managed to complete all the work by the promised hour. They had everything packed up and were on their way before the new inn guests' scheduled arrival.

Louise got home shortly after the crew left.

"How did your day go?" Jane asked, meeting her at the front door.

"Oh, the judge adjourned for the day two hours ago, but Florence had some errands in Potterston. We had to stop at a florist shop to arrange flowers for a banquet she's chairing, then pick up some shoes she'd left to be repaired. And there's a market on the edge of town that sells whole roasted chickens. She wanted to buy one since she wouldn't have much time to fix dinner."

"It doesn't sound like ride-sharing is working out very well," Jane sympathized.

"Well, I hope it will only be a few more days. I'm afraid her feelings would be hurt if I backed out of carpooling. It is energy efficient, but I hope she's done all her errands for this week. How did the cleaning go?"

"Very well. There was a lot of hustle and bustle all day, but everything I've seen so far looks splendid. I haven't checked the upstairs rooms yet."

"Is Cynthia here?"

"No, she hasn't returned from the library."

"I have an idea," Louise said. "Why don't we all go out for dinner this evening? It would be a relaxing end to a hectic day."

"I'd love to," Jane said, "but I'm expecting guests to arrive any time between now and perhaps seven o'clock. They live near Cleveland and weren't exactly sure when they would get here. Anyway, I have vegetable lasagna—garlic free—that only needs to be heated in the oven. I noticed that Joanna usually leaves more on her plate than she eats, but I thought that she might be tempted by a vegetarian dish."

"The rooms upstairs look lovely," Alice said, coming down the stairs. "I was puttering a bit in the attic. Someday that will need a thorough cleaning too, but I imagine we'll have to do it together."

"So that's where you were," Jane said. "I was afraid the cleaners had driven you out of the house."

"Well, I did go out earlier for a needed walk. Then I relaxed on the porch until I got the idea of going to the attic. What can I do to help with dinner?"

Jane almost rejected her help, but she realized in time that Alice needed to be helpful.

"You can set the table for a clean-house celebration. It will have to be in the kitchen, though. The carpet in the dining room is still damp."

Dinner was over and the table cleared before the new guests arrived. Louise and Cynthia had gone for a walk, and Alice had invited Joanna to join her in the parlor to discuss the project at the library.

Jane met the couple in the newly polished foyer.

"Mr. and Mrs.Wallace?" she asked, greeting them with a smile.

"Yes, but please call us Ross and Margo," the large, powerfully built man said.

"Jane Howard, I'm pleased to meet you. I hope you'll enjoy your stay at Grace Chapel Inn."

"Such a lovely name," his diminutive wife said.

"My father was the minister at Grace Chapel. You may have noticed it on your way here. This was our family home."

"How wonderful of you to share it." Margo Wallace had a small voice that matched her petite size. Her light brown hair was cut short and muted by a mix of gray. Luminous blue eyes were set in a heart-shaped, elfin face.

Jane went behind the desk and prepared to register them.

"I understand you want to stay until a week from Sunday, the twenty-fifth."

"That's not entirely certain," Margo said with a slight frown. "We could be called home sooner."

"That's unlikely, so plan on our staying," her husband said mildly to Jane, then addressed his wife. "Penny is eighteen. She'll do just fine without us for a few days."

"Our daughter has a part-time job," Margo explained to Jane. "She's starting college in August, and she's determined to earn some spending money on her own. Usually she loves to come with us on our bird-watching expeditions."

"She's with her grandmother," Ross said. "The two of them will have a great time together."

"Yes, I suppose so," his wife said.

"So you're bird-watchers," Jane said. "I just installed a new feeder in the backyard. It was on sale, and so I thought I'd get it and set it up, though I'll usually only stock it in the winter. I love seeing the different varieties that show up."

"We go in all seasons," Margo said enthusiastically. "We love hiking and cross-country skiing, so not much slows us down."

Jane was glad the garden room was available for them. They seemed like a couple who would enjoy looking out at her flower beds, some of them now in bloom with daffodils and tulips. It also had the best view for bird-watchers, although she didn't know whether they would see any unusual ones near the inn.

"We had a cleaning service working here today," Jane explained. "I believe your room has aired out by now."

"Oh, the scent of a clean room won't bother us at all," Margo assured her.

She led them upstairs, and the couple admired the room, decorated in shades of green with a floral border along the wainscoting and at the ceiling, and agreed that a seven o'clock breakfast would suit them just fine.

Jane went back to the kitchen, pleased at the prospect of interesting conversations with the bird-watchers. Although she welcomed all their guests and enjoyed providing hospitality, it was especially gratifying to host people who shared her interests. She'd never bird-watched in any organized way, but she found birds and their habits fascinating. She looked forward to learning more about the Wallaces' hobby.

Chapter Eight 

When Jane took her golden-brown soufflé au fromage from the oven, she decided it was well worth getting up a little earlier to make it. The dish had risen to perfection, and the imported cheddar spiced by the hints of cayenne and nutmeg filled the kitchen with fragrance.

Mr. and Mrs. Wallace were already in the dining room, enjoying a fruit compote she'd prepared the night before. They were coffee drinkers, so she had brewed a savory Columbian blend and placed the pot on a warming tray for them to help themselves as often as they liked.

To complement the soufflé, she took thin slices of a hard-crusted bread purchased at the bakery, lightly brushed olive oil on both sides and toasted them under the oven broiler. Although she had put tart cherry jam and a translucent apple jelly on the table, she much preferred the crispy toast on its own.

She carried the high-sided white porcelain soufflé dish to the dining room, using heavy quilted mitts to protect her hands. Serving it at the table was more dramatic than dishing it out in the kitchen, and, as a professional chef, she knew that presentation was an important part of enjoying a gourmet meal.

"My goodness, I wasn't expecting anything like this," Margo Wallace said. "You make us feel so special."

She was dressed for the day in a scaled-down version of a bush jacket and knee-length walking shorts with hiking boots that seemed too heavy for her slender legs. Her husband Ross wore jeans and a soccer jersey, and his boots were definitely trail-worthy.

Jane dished out generous portions, then put the remainder on the warmer beside the coffee.

"Please help yourself to seconds," she said as she passed the toast.

"Won't you join us?" Margo asked.

"Thank you, but I'll have breakfast when my sisters come down."

"Have a cup of coffee then," Ross urged. "Best brew I've tasted in ages."

"We want to tell you about our plans," his wife urged.

Jane was curious to know what was involved in a bird-watching expedition, so she joined the couple at the table.

"Where are you going? Acorn Hill isn't near a bird sanctuary."

"No, but we wanted to stay at a place that was centrally located to the areas we intend to visit," Ross said.

"Packing up and finding new lodging every night is such a chore," Margo said. "Ross investigated bed-and-breakfasts, and your inn sounded like exactly what we wanted, a home away from home."

"I hope we live up to your expectations," Jane said.

"It's nice and quiet here," Margo said. "I slept better than I expected, considering that our daughter is on my mind. The room and the bed are wonderfully comfy."

"Honey, we're going to have a great time. We were both overdue for a vacation, and it's good that Penny made her own plans. The work experience will be great."

"I know." His wife smiled weakly. "It's just that she's leaving us for good."

"Hardly that." Ross turned to Jane and explained, "Our daughter is going to an out-of-state college. She's a top student and has a great scholarship."

"The house will be so empty," his wife said sadly.

"Your job keeps you busy, and she will be home for school breaks."

"Where do you work?" Jane asked.

"I'm a paralegal," Margo told her. "The lawyer I work for was a good friend of my father's."

"I'm sure that must be very interesting work," Jane said.

"Yes, it can be. I really enjoy it."

Jane finished her coffee and started to get up, but Ross stopped her.

"Wait, we haven't told you about our schedule," he said enthusiastically. "This is a great state for bird-watching. Hundreds of species call it home, and even more migrate through it."

"I believe the most accurate count is 418 species," Margo said. "There's such a great diversity of habitats here: three river systems, lakes, swamps, bogs, marshes and farmland. It's a nesting paradise and an important stop along the Atlantic Flyway."

"That's a migration route," Ross explained. "What makes this state especially great for bird-watchers are the parks and sanctuaries."

"There's Cook Forest and Clear Creek State Park. We've been to Erie National Wildlife Sanctuary and loved it. Then there's Hawk Mountain Sanctuary and Timberdoodle Flats Trail."

"This is your state. You probably know all about them," Ross said.

"It's a big state," Jane said, a bit overwhelmed by the visitors' knowledge of Pennsylvania's nature spots. She had to get out of the kitchen more often.

"Actually, we're on a quest," Margo said, pausing to take a bite of the soufflé. "We've never seen a Henslow's sparrow."

"It's very rare. We'd love to be able to go back to our local bird-watching club and report that we saw one."

"I've never even heard of it," Jane admitted.

"They're secretive little rascals," Ross explained. "Like to perch on low branches to sing their songs."

"I have a special fondness for tiny birds like the black-capped chickadee and the tufted titmouse. They have to survive in a world filled with aggressive black crows and blue jays." Margo laughed at herself. "I get a bit fanciful sometimes. I like to make up stories about birds."

"Did I hear you say 'stories about birds'?" Cynthia appeared in the doorway to the dining room. "Sorry to interrupt, but my curiosity got the better of me."

"Ross and Margo Wallace, this is my niece Cynthia Smith. She's staying with us while her editorial offices in Boston are being renovated."

"Oh, you're an editor," Margo said enthusiastically. "Please, come join us. What do you edit?"

"Children's books," Cynthia said, slipping onto a vacant chair. "In fact, I edited a story that followed a family of Canadian geese on their annual migration. It was very popular with readers ages seven to ten."

"It's wonderful for young children to develop an interest in the habits of birds," Margo said. "We started taking our daughter Penny on bird-watching trips when she still needed to be carried on her father's back. This is the first trip in a long time that she didn't come with us."

"Got herself a part-time job at the local drugstore. She has it in mind that she might want to be a pharmacist."

"Ross and Margo are going to do some bird-watching," Jane said. "They'll be with us through next week."

"I hope to see more of you then," Cynthia said, rising from the chair.

"I would love to hear more about the books you edit," Margo said. "I've been making up stories about birds most of my life, but I wouldn't know how to go about putting them down on paper."

"Published authors have told me that they felt the same way at the beginning of their careers. I always suggest taking a writing course or joining a writers' group."

"How could I find one?"

"You could start on the Internet or ask your local librarian for help. There are many good books and several magazines for writers too."

"Even if I could write one of my stories in a way someone might want to read, I wouldn't know how to get it printed.

Wouldn't I have to go to New York City and find an agent or something?"

"Not at all. There are special books telling you how to sell what you write and listing all the freelance markets. I won't tell you that it's easy to get started. Some authors work for years to get published, but perseverance can pay off."

"I'm so glad I've met you," Margo said earnestly. "I hope to see more of you."

"Thank you. I look forward to visiting with you," Cynthia said.

After the Wallaces left, Jane joined Cynthia in the kitchen.

"I'm glad you talked to her about writing. She's feeling down about her daughter's going away to college. She needs a distraction."

"Oh, Aunt Jane, I can't tell you how often I meet people who want to be writers. I can't go to a social event—or even a dentist's appointment—without running into someone who has an urge to write. The last time I had my teeth cleaned, the hygienist talked nonstop about an idea she had for a book. I don't like to discourage anyone. There are people out there with talent and ideas that should be developed, but it's not fair to make it sound easy."

"I thought you gave her good answers."

"Thanks. Of course, most people are just curious. They have no intention of trying to write anything, and most often they don't have the time or self-discipline to be successful writers. Am I too late for breakfast?"

"Certainly not. What would you like? You used to like my apple pancakes."

"I love all your cooking, Aunt Jane, but you don't need to fix a big breakfast for me. I'm happy with a bowl of cereal."

"You and your mother," Jane teased. "I think you'd both skip out without anything if I let you."

"Has Mother come down yet?"

"She's here now," Louise said, coming into the kitchen. "I only have five minutes before Florence picks me up. Do you have a granola bar I can take with me?"

"Mother, you need more than that to fortify yourself for court," Cynthia said with a big smile.

"What I need is to be there on time. I just couldn't seem to get moving this morning. I've gotten out of the habit of needing to be somewhere first thing in the morning."

Louise was trying her hardest to get beyond any personal feelings about the defendant, Edward Reddenhurst. She'd prayed in her room before going downstairs that morning. Meditation had cleared her mind of the bad impression he'd made on her.

When the jury filed into the courtroom for the fourth day of the trial, she tried to avoid staring at Reddenhurst. It was difficult, since his profile was directly in her line of vision. He wasn't elderly by any measurement, but his face was leathery, perhaps from too much tanning. Deep lines ran from the corners of his mouth to the sides of his nose, but there were still hints that he'd been handsome in his younger years. What was off-putting to Louise was his arrogance. Far from showing any sign of guilt or repentance, he projected anger and a sense that he was surrounded by inferiors.

He glanced at the jury, regarding them with a dark, stony gaze. Louise shivered, wrapping her arms across her chest.

"It is cold in here, isn't it?" Eve Franken whispered to her. "I wonder whether they've turned the air conditioning too low."

Louise was saved from answering when they were all asked to rise for the judge's entrance. There was no way she could explain to another juror that her little shudder had nothing to do with the temperature.

It was Harry's turn to begin presenting witnesses for the defense. Unlike his partners, who wore dark suits, white shirts and conservative ties, he looked casual in tasseled loafers, chinos and a sports jacket with leather patches on the elbows. Maybe he dressed that way to emphasize his more relaxed technique in handling a witness.

His appearance was deceptive. He had a keen intellect and was quick to underscore anything said by the prosecution witness—an executive of the corporation that now owned the department store—that could be helpful to the defendant. Several times the prosecutor objected to the line of questioning, but so far, the judge had ruled in Harry's favor.

Louise noticed something a bit odd. Reddenhurst kept looking over his shoulder at the benches behind him. She followed his gaze, seeing only a scattering of spectators. Then she realized why Reddenhurst kept looking. The stylishly dressed woman who had been there every day since the beginning of the trial hadn't put in an appearance yet.

Every five or ten minutes the defendant looked behind him to check the audience. When he didn't see the woman, his shoulders slumped in his beautifully fitted gray silk suit, and he stared down at the table in front of him. It was the first time Louise had seen a chink in his armor, and she was surprised to feel a glimmer of sympathy for him. His wife, if that was who the missing woman was, had apparently let him down by not coming today. Was she the reason for his alleged embezzlement? Was this a sign that she was loyal to him only when he had the means to treat her lavishly?

Louise knew she had to put this speculation out of her mind. It had nothing to do with his guilt or innocence, but it served to remind her that she was going to have to decide the fate of a vulnerable human being, not the villain she'd been creating in her mind. She forced her attention back to the witness.

After nearly two hours of cross-examination, the prosecutor got the witness to admit that he personally disliked Reddenhurst and held a grudge against him for an incident in the past that had nothing to do with the alleged embezzlement. It wasn't much of an admission in Louise's opinion, but it did suggest that the witness might have an ulterior motive for his testimony.

When it was her turn again Ms. Gottschek managed to minimize the damage to her case. She was shrewd enough not to play games with the defense attorneys, and her businesslike attitude was impressive. Louise didn't know whether it would be enough to counteract the barrage of contrary evidence coming from Tom, Dick and Harry, but the prosecutor was proving to be a worthy opponent.

The lunch break couldn't have been more welcome. One thing the jury did agree on already as they sat down to eat was that a morning in court was exhausting. How much more information would they have to absorb before they had to make a decision?

"My head is just plain spinning," Eve said.

"Well, it's all a waste of my time," Yvonne Woodbury, the real-estate salesperson, said. "He's guilty as sin. I say lock him away and good riddance."

She was a stringy, rather colorless woman who favored black suits and dresses worn with ropey strings of beads or pearls. Yvonne had already made it clear that no penalty was too harsh for a reprobate like Reddenhurst. The bailiff had had to admonish her several times for voicing her opinion in public. If the rest of the jury voted to acquit, she was the most likely to be a holdout.

Louise wondered, not for the first time, whether anyone among them would be so adamant about his innocence. Was this a group of people who would weigh every fact in a fair and impartial way? She was struggling herself to put aside any bias she might feel toward the defendant.

It was particularly hard that she couldn't talk over the evidence with Jane and Alice.

The last thing Alice wanted to do was prevent Joanna from doing her work for the publisher, but over their breakfast together, she did

bring up the idea of helping at the library. They were the last ones to eat this morning, and the younger woman seemed inclined to linger, chatting about a poem she was writing that praised the joys of small-town life. Her response to Alice's tentative suggestion was more than enthusiastic.

"What a wonderful idea! I would adore reading aloud. When I was little, our town's librarian was the one who got me interested in reading. She started me on fiction and then introduced me to poetry. I still remember the first poem I memorized. I hated having to go to bed early, so I really identified with Robert Louis Stevenson's 'Bed in Summer.' I can still see the little book *A Child's Garden of Verses*. It was illustrated with silhouettes of children dressed in period clothing."

"I remember that poem," Alice said, "but I can't remember exactly how it goes."

Not surprisingly, Joanna began reciting it:

"*In winter I get up at night*
And dress by yellow candle-light.
In summer, quite the other way,
I have to go to bed by day."

"Of course, I don't want to interfere with your work," Alice was quick to say. "The children won't be coming until afternoon when school is out. If you wouldn't mind working especially hard in the morning and early afternoon—"

"No problem," Joanna said emphatically. "I'll work like crazy until it's time to go to the library."

"In that case," Alice said, smiling at her eagerness, "why don't you hurry and get your work done. Then we can go talk to the librarian later in the day."

"That will give me an incentive to get a lot done today."

Alice thought her idea might work, if indeed Joanna did make good use of her time that day.

Four o'clock came, and, amazingly, Joanna was waiting on the front porch to walk to the library. Alice seemed to detect a jaunty spring in her steps, and she'd even abandoned her flip-flops for a pair of canvas slip-ons, not high-tech walking shoes but certainly an improvement.

Once she'd introduced Joanna to Nia, Alice wandered off to look at the mystery shelves, giving both young women a chance to get acquainted and to discuss the program. She found a detective story by one of her favorite authors and decided to check it out, taking it to the desk manned by one of the library's part-time workers. Joanna and the librarian were still in conference, so Alice sat to begin reading her book. Surprisingly, she'd finished a whole chapter before Joanna was ready to go back to the inn.

"She's going to talk to the ANGELs about my idea," Joanna said with unusual animation in her voice.

Alice expected to hear about the plan, but Joanna was uncharacteristically close-mouthed. She didn't press her, not wanting to deprive her of the pleasure of having a secret. She could rely on Nia to coordinate with the ANGELs. The young librarian was extremely skillful when it came to public relations, so none of Alice's girls would feel left out.

Jane's kitchen had never seemed so welcoming as it did when Louise got home from her day in court. Her sister was working on horseradish dressing to go on her spinach, tomato and red onion salad.

"What's for dinner?" Louise asked, not ready to say anything about her day.

"I'm baking red snapper fillets, Florida style. It's been a challenge to do whole meals without a trace of garlic, but this recipe only calls for black pepper, nutmeg and lemon rind. I had thought an Asian dish would be nice, lots of noodles and vegetables, but every soy and teriyaki sauce I could find has garlic as an ingredient. So do Worcestershire and ninety-nine percent of all salad dressings."

Louise suspected that Jane was talking food to give her time to wind down, and she certainly needed it. The testimony had gotten terribly technical in the afternoon, but she wasn't going to try to sort it out in her head right now. What bothered her was the image of Edward Reddenhurst as a man in pain.

Until today, he'd seemed arrogant and self-assured, as though the charges against him were just minor irritations. Apparently he had great faith in his legal team. What seemed to shake him was the absence of the stylish woman. When the jury was leaving the building for lunch, Louise had seen him hunched over a cell phone in the corridor, speaking in a low, urgent tone. She caught a few words, enough to confirm that he was calling the woman about her absence in the courtroom that day. There had been even fewer spectators that afternoon, and she was not among them.

Louise recalled how he had slumped at the table, seemingly uninterested in the proceedings. She tried to rein in her imagination, but she wondered whether he had stolen from the business and the foundation in order to keep the woman happy. Certainly she was younger than he and probably high-maintenance, judging from her expensive jewelry and clothes and her chic hairstyle.

"Don't you think so?" Jane asked.

She'd lost the thread of Jane's conversation. "I'm sorry. I still had the trial on my mind," she confessed. "What was it you were saying?"

Jane laughed. "I should know you have more important decisions to make than whether to eat in the kitchen or the dining room."

"Either is fine," Louise said with an apologetic smile, and then she excused herself to go freshen up for dinner.

By the time she returned to the kitchen, everyone else had gathered around the table.

As they enjoyed another of Jane's delicious meals, Louise listened fondly to Cynthia's account of her day, one spent reading unsolicited manuscripts.

"I've found one that has some potential," she said. "We might even be able to buy it if the author is willing to make major changes."

"Wouldn't any writer be happy to do that for a chance to be published?" Jane asked, passing a plate of homemade potato rolls.

"You would think so," Cynthia said, "but some authors, particularly unseasoned ones, are so devoted to every word they've written that it's impossible to work with them. It's a shame, really. Good writers never stop honing their craft. There's always something new to learn. That's true in my job too."

A muted ring interrupted their conversation, and Jane jumped up to answer the phone.

"It's for you, Alice," she said, handing the kitchen phone to her sister.

"Oh, hello, Jenny. No, it's perfectly all right. We've nearly finished dinner."

Alice listened for some time, then soothingly assured the young girl that everything would work out.

"Don't worry. You can get back on schedule after the concert," she said before saying good-bye.

"We've had a little wrinkle in the library program," she said, returning to her place at the table. "Several of the girls who signed up to work next week are in the school choir. Their director has scheduled after-school practices because they have a big spring concert coming up. They're really very good—they've won awards in competitions. Still it's a shame they'll miss some of the library project. They were really looking forward to working with children, but I suppose we can postpone the start until after the concert."

"You don't need to do that," Joanna said excitedly. "I'll help with the children next week."

"We have quite a few signed up," Alice said. "It might be a bigger job than you want to take on."

"The more, the merrier. I have loads of ideas. It will be so much fun."

Louise saw her sister exchange a look with Cynthia.

"I wouldn't want to interfere with your editing work," Alice said.

"Oh, there's plenty of time to get that done and do the program at the library too. I work better under pressure. Maybe I'll read the book I'm editing and see how the children react to it. I know I can come up with some great crafts. I went to camp every summer for years when I was a kid. We were always gluing or weaving or carving something."

"These children are too young for knives," Alice said, looking a bit worried.

"Of course," Joanna said with a little laugh, apparently not taking offense at the warning. "I'll be sure that whatever we do will be age appropriate."

"I'll talk to Nia Komonos tomorrow. It will be her decision," Alice said.

She smiled, but Louise knew her sister too well to be fooled. She wasn't convinced that the program should go ahead without some of the key ANGELs who had planned it.

Chapter Nine 

A bird was chirping outside Louise's bedroom window, and she couldn't think of a nicer way to be awakened. It was pleasant not to be summoned by the harsh buzz of her alarm clock and even sweeter to know that it was Sunday, a day of worship and rest.

Saturday had been lovely. She and Cynthia had gone to Potterston to shop. They'd had lunch at a new Thai restaurant that featured a noon buffet, and it had more than lived up to its excellent reviews.

The evening had been pleasant too. It wasn't often that the whole family could have a long, leisurely conversation, catching up on everything that had been happening in their lives. She felt a little sad that Joanna had excused herself to go to her room alone, especially since they had all tried to include her in the conversation. But perhaps quiet time to work on her own poetry was a treat for the young editor.

Louise was glad of the break from jury duty, but she was surprised to feel an unexpected bond with the other jurors. Her experience in court was like no other in her life. Except for Florence, she might never see any of these people again, yet they were forging relationships, however temporary, that most of them wouldn't forget for a long time. For some, this was possibly the first time that their opinions would be valued. They would have to come together with one mind in order to make a decision. Louise could only compare the jury situation to strangers caught up in a crisis.

The young man with the lawn service was impatient to be finished with the trial. Did that mean he would go along with any decision the group made?

Yvonne had already decided that Reddenhurst deserved severe punishment. Eve and Mona Hill, the bank teller, had developed a friendship. Did that mean they would both vote the same way?

It was possible that some jurors would have a hard time making up their minds, especially Sterling Hagar, the accountant who seemed to weigh every word that was said to him, even casual comments at lunch.

Whatever happened with the trial next week, Louise resolved to put it out of her mind for now. After her devotions and a quick shower, she slipped into a dress she had worn only once, for Easter. It was a flattering lightweight blue knit with a crossover neckline and a gently flowing skirt. She'd intended to save the dress for special occasions like concerts, but she felt like celebrating the Lord's Day and the time with her loved ones.

"My, don't you look lovely," Alice said when Louise joined the others in the dining room. "That color goes so well with your eyes."

"Thank you. Are the guests sleeping late this morning?"

"Not at all," Jane explained. "They left without breakfast at the crack of dawn to meet some friends for a day of bird-watching."

"Joanna went upstairs to change," Cynthia said. "She wants to come to church with us."

"That will be nice."

Louise helped herself to cranberry juice and a warm bran muffin from the buffet. Split and lightly buttered, a muffin was one of her favorite morning treats. Because their only guests had not wanted breakfast, Jane had laid out a casual buffet breakfast: a variety of quick breads, sweet rolls, fruit juice and hot beverages.

"I've invited a few friends for Sunday dinner," Jane said. "Viola, Rev. Thompson and Nia Komonos. I'm experimenting with a Greek menu in her honor. Fortunately I found some good recipes that don't require garlic."

"What are you making?" Louise asked.

"You'll have to wait and see." Jane smiled and busied herself clearing the buffet. "Let me put the cream cheese and butter in the fridge. Then I'll be ready to go."

"It's taking Joanna a long time," Cynthia said with the sigh of resignation that often crept into her voice when she was talking about her coworker. "You three go ahead so you're not late. I know you like to warm up the organ a bit, Mother. I'll wait for her."

"I'll be happy to wait too. I have some time," Louise said.

"No, Mother, go without me. No doubt she'll be down any minute."

Louise noted that she and her sisters were actually a bit early when they got to the chapel. Members of the congregation were visiting outside the church door and talking in small groups. She saw Florence in animated conversation with several other women. When Florence spotted Louise, she hurried toward her.

"I've had the most amazing insights into the trial," she said somewhat breathlessly. "There's nothing like a little distance to clarify troubling points."

"That's reassuring," Louise said, trying to keep disapproval out of her voice. "But do you really think we should discuss it here?"

"Oh, I'm sure the members of our congregation wouldn't try to influence my vote," Florence said, straightening the jacket of her daintily flowered peach linen suit.

Louise couldn't help reminding her of the instructions that they had received. "You know we're not supposed to discuss the case."

"I didn't take that to mean we can't talk to each other," she said a bit indignantly. "After all, we're both jurors."

"Truthfully, Florence, I was hoping to put the case out of my mind today. Just not think about it."

"Oh, I understand. That way you can start fresh tomorrow. Do you think there will be more testimony?"

"I hope not," Louise said, wishing that the case would end soon, a desire that Florence didn't share. In fact, her cojuror was having the time of her life. Louise believed that Florence's role on the jury made her feel important and needed. If she had to guess, Louise would say Florence was leaning toward conviction.

She saw her daughter and Joanna moving toward the church and excused herself to meet them.

"Good morning, Joanna. I'm so happy you decided to join us. I think you'll enjoy Rev. Thompson's sermon."

"Cynthia has been telling me all about him, that he's from Boston and that his wife died tragically from a heart condition. How sad to be a widower at such a young age. Do you think he'll ever find love again?"

"He has great love for the Lord and for the church," Louise said, not wanting to discuss their minister's personal life. She was surprised that Cynthia had shared his story, but then, Joanna had a way of extracting information.

Louise left Cynthia and Joanna and went into the church to prepare the organ. She found her tension slipping away as it so often did when she took her place on the bench and soon began the opening hymn.

Rev. Thompson began his sermon by reading Psalm 1, which concluded:

> *"For the* Lord *watches over the way of the righteous,*
> *but the way of the wicked will perish"* (1:6).

The pastor always stressed the positive in his sermons, and today he brought to life a beloved biblical image of the righteous person who was "like a tree planted by streams of water, which yields its fruit in season and whose leaf does not wither."

It always amazed Louise that he could take a single thought and apply it to the lives of everyone in the congregation. The second verse of the psalm states that the righteous man finds "delight in the law of the Lord." In essence, Louise decided, the common law that was the basis of justice in modern courts looked to the heritage of the Bible. It attempted to distinguish between right and wrong, to protect the innocent and punish the guilty.

When the last notes of the recessional hymn died out, Louise moved quickly from behind the organ and toward the door in an effort to avoid Florence. Undoubtedly her fellow juror would have something to say about sinners and the need to punish the wicked. The last thing Louise wanted was to debate the meaning of the psalm with her.

"What a wonderful sermon," Joanna said as all of them were walking home together. "I love the poetry in the Bible. I've tried using parallelism as the Hebrews did, but it's more difficult than it looks. Imagine the person who wrote a line like: 'They will beat their swords into plowshares and their spears into pruning hooks' [Isaiah 2:4]. It makes me shiver to say it."

"'Nation will not take up sword against nation, nor will they train for war anymore,'" Cynthia said, completing the thought.

"That's synonymous parallelism," Joanna said, her eyes sparkling with enthusiasm. "Sometimes parallelism does the opposite. The second part is the antithesis of the first thought. One that sticks with me is 'A wise son brings joy to his father, but a foolish son grief to his mother' [Proverbs 10:1]. My mother liked to say that, only she was talking about her daughter—namely me—not her son. Do you know how hard it is to grow up with a perfect sibling?"

Jane giggled a little at her wistful comment. "Try having two perfect sisters. I always seemed to be the one who got into trouble."

"Nonsense, you were a lovely child," Alice assured her.

"Sweet as pie," Louise teased, "except when someone tried to rein in your tomboy ways. I never could understand your attraction to treetops."

"I liked to look for birds' nests, not to disturb them, just to see the eggs," Jane explained. "In fact, I still like to, but I'm content to do it from the ground. Who would cook if I fell out of a tree?"

Louise had been so interested in their conversation that the short walk home seemed to take no time at all. She hoped that Joanna would feel free to share more of her thoughts at dinner. She was certainly full of surprises. The younger woman was many things, but seldom dull.

Alice felt a glow of pleasure that her faith in Joanna seemed to be justified. The woman lacked focus regarding things that didn't interest her, but her depth of understanding when it came to words and ideas was truly impressive.

After changing into crisply pleated nutmeg-brown slacks and a new tunic in shades of amber and gold, Alice did a few personal chores, then gravitated to the kitchen where Jane was busy preparing dinner for their company.

"I love an early afternoon dinner party," Alice said. "It's such a nice time to entertain. People are still fresh, not tired from a full day. What can I do to help you?"

"You can set the table in the dining room. Use our best china and the crystal goblets for water. I've already put out a clean tablecloth."

"Let's see, there's five of us plus Viola, Nia and Rev. Thompson, eight in all."

"Nine. Aunt Ethel is coming too."

"Of course, it wouldn't be a party without her. And I'm sure she's at loose ends with Lloyd Tynan out of town." Alice was referring to Ethel's special friend, the mayor of Acorn Hill. "What are you preparing for dinner?"

"Don't you want to be surprised?" Jane teased.

"No, I'm too intrigued to wait. I'm guessing long grain white rice is on the menu, since it's sitting on the counter."

"Yes, I'm making Greek rice pilaf. I'll cook the rice in butter and chicken broth, season with salt, pepper and cinnamon, and add yellow raisins and slivered almonds."

"Sounds yummy, but what about the main course?"

"Souvlakia."

"I don't have a clue what that is."

"Chicken breasts, marinated in mustard, sage, honey and olive oil, then grilled on skewers along with skewers of Kalamata olives. The chicken and the olives are served on a bed of whole-wheat bread crumbs sautéed with shallots, sage and chives. Some chefs use pine nuts too, but I couldn't find any when I went shopping."

"What an interesting dish."

"I haven't made it since I worked in the restaurant. But that's all I'm going to tell you. There have to be a few surprises."

Viola arrived at the back door and went straight into the kitchen with the familiarity of an old friend. Jane was putting the finishing touches on her Greek red cabbage salad, topping it with feta cheese and olives. She liked to add the cheese at the last minute, since the cabbage would dye it red if it sat too long. Because the meal was rather rich, she opted to serve a long loaf of Italian bread, cutting slices down to the bottom crust so the diners could pull them off in tasty, hard-crusted chunks.

She had made baklava the day before. She always enjoyed working with the delicate phyllo pastry leaves, keeping them under a damp cloth while she worked to prevent them from becoming dry. She'd layered the dough with sugar and chopped pistachios. Then she poured over the filled dough a sugar syrup flavored with lemon juice and orange blossom water. She preferred the syrup's lighter flavor to the traditional honey. The dessert was best if it sat for twenty-four hours after baking, so hers would be at the peak of perfection.

"Is there anything I can do?" Viola asked.

"Really, there's nothing to do, but thank you for offering," Jane said. "Why don't you join the others in the parlor? Louise and Cynthia are playing some duets. Aunt Ethel and Rev. Thompson are with them, and I think Nia Komonos is here too."

All their guests except Joanna were in the parlor enjoying the impromptu recital, so Jane brought out her Greek dip—yogurt flavored with mustard, honey, dill, thyme and pepper. She was serving it with a platter of prawns and crisp fresh vegetables. Alice helped her by carrying individual plates and napkins into the parlor, where a table was ready to serve the appetizers.

"I hope Joanna hasn't forgotten the time," Alice said.

Cynthia left the piano bench while Louise continued to play soft background music.

"I'll go check on her," she said. "I know she was excited about discussing psalms with Rev. Thompson."

"I can do it," Alice offered.

"No, you relax," Cynthia said with a warm smile for her aunt. "I'll go remind her that dinner is ready."

Cynthia returned from her search for Joanna several minutes later and shrugged helplessly at her aunt.

"I went over the house, top to bottom," she told Alice in a low voice. "No sign of Joanna, and she isn't anywhere in the vicinity of the inn. I'm at a loss to know where to look next. I can only hope that she'll show up eventually." Cynthia let out a sigh.

"Well, don't let it spoil the gathering for you," Alice said.

Joanna had seemed quite keen on the dinner party, so it was odd that she wasn't there. Alice thought of taking the car to look for her, but it was highly unlikely that she could find her that way. Torn between irritation and concern, she went to the kitchen to speak to Jane.

"The souvlakia is a last-minute dish. I don't know whether to delay longer or grill the chicken now," Jane said.

As flexible as her sister was as a chef, Alice knew that Jane didn't like to keep guests waiting.

"Why don't you go ahead, and I'll remove Joanna's place setting from the table. If she does come while we're eating, I can always return it," Alice suggested.

"I guess that's best," Jane reluctantly agreed.

The dinner was lovely and the guests appreciative, but Alice's pleasure was dulled by concern for Joanna. She didn't believe the younger woman meant to be discourteous. She simply couldn't keep her mind on track when it came to ordinary activities. Cynthia wasn't worried by her absence, however, and she knew her better than anyone. Apparently Joanna had a bad habit of disappearing at work, too, and that habit was one of the reasons why her job was on the line now. Still, she would have enjoyed the lively and stimulating conversation even though food didn't much interest her.

When their guests had left and the cleanup was done, Alice took the mystery novel she'd been reading and settled down on her favorite chair on the front porch. She couldn't seem to concentrate on the story, though, and her eyes kept straying to the street, expecting to see Joanna padding along in her flip-flops.

She dozed, awaking with a start as Joanna came up the front steps.

"Oh, Joanna, we missed you at dinner," she said.

"I'm so sorry," she said a bit breathlessly. "By the time I remembered, it was way past the time Jane told me."

"Where have you been?" Alice knew that she wasn't Joanna's keeper, but she couldn't imagine what the woman had been doing in Acorn Hill on a Sunday afternoon.

"A poem has been going round and round in my head for ages, but I never hit on quite the right form for it. When I heard the psalm in church, it came to me. I had to write it immediately, before it escaped me."

"It must have been quite a long poem. You've been gone for hours."

"Not so long," Joanna said a bit vaguely. "Finding just the right words is hard."

"Wherever did you find to work?" Alice knew the library was closed, as were other places where she might have holed up to write.

"Oh, I just walked until I found a little woods with a fallen tree. I sat on the log and wrote in my notebook. I'm afraid I lost all track of time. Then when I started back, I made a wrong turn. A boy riding his bike showed me the way to the inn, and here I am, footsore but happy that I finally finished the poem. I wanted it to be special, and I think it is."

Joanna seemed so pleased about what she'd written that Alice instantly forgave her, even though the young woman had given her a scare by being gone so long. Joanna pulled up a chair next to Alice and sat down. "My feet hurt. I'm not used to walking on country roads."

Alice wanted to point out that flips-flops were hardly hiking shoes in any locale, but she didn't want to burst Joanna's bubble of happiness. Her face was more animated than it had been at any time since arriving at the inn.

"Well, I'm glad you're back now. Would you like some dinner? I'm sure Jane has all kinds of leftovers."

"I don't want to be a bother."

"Fixing food is never a bother to my sister. Would you like me to bring a tray out here for you?"

"No, please, I can't let you wait on me. Maybe I can just make myself something simple like a cheese sandwich."

Alice laughed softly. "I can't imagine something so plain coming out of Jane's kitchen. Let's go see what she has in the fridge."

She led the way over Joanna's protests, finding the kitchen deserted.

In the fridge she located a generous portion of Greek salad and a serving of souvlakia and rice pilaf in a porcelain dish suitable for the microwave. It looked as if Jane had spooned a bit of extra chicken broth over it to prevent drying as it heated. It was only the work of a few minutes to put a nice meal in front of Joanna.

"I feel terrible for putting you to so much trouble." For once Joanna tackled a meal with gusto. "I would like to dedicate a poem to you and your sisters, but not the one I wrote today. That one's about my family."

"Oh?" Alice was curious, but she didn't want to intrude on Joanna's personal thoughts.

"It was the line in Proverbs 10 about a wise son bringing joy to his father. My parents always seemed to approve of everything my brother Jock did. He loved the sea and couldn't wait until he was old enough to help my father fish. He still works on one of Dad's fishing boats, and it's the only life he wants. I was the maverick. Nothing I did was quite what my parents wanted for their daughter."

Alice nodded sympathetically.

"I had to leave Maine." There was pain in her voice. "There just wasn't anything there. You can't imagine. My mother was already speculating about marriage, pointing out different boys in town that she thought were good prospects. I could never explain that I didn't want the kind of life they had to offer." Joanna absentmindedly took a bite of salad.

"I wanted to explain how I felt, but my parents never seemed to have time to listen. I'm ashamed to say that I envied Jock. He was always the favorite child, but why wouldn't he be? He never disappointed them. He wanted to do exactly what they expected. I was the oddball in the family."

"That must have been hard."

Joanna paused, giving exaggerated attention to the food in front of her. She ate a few bites and continued talking.

"I resented it. I know that makes me seem shallow."

"You're anything but that," Alice assured her.

"I had to forgive myself for being different and forgive my parents for not accepting me as I am. I think I've done that now. That's what my poem is about. Does that sound terribly strange to you?"

"Not at all. It sounds very healthy, just the kind of thinking that could benefit many people. I think it's good that you've written a poem to share your feelings with others."

"I'm not quite ready to let anyone read it."

"That's understandable. You wrote it for yourself."

"It's probably the best thing I've ever written. Someday I

would like to see it in print. I'd like my parents to see it, too, when I'm ready."

"When you're ready," Alice repeated, a bit awed that Joanna had shared so much with her.

She felt amazingly close to her at this moment and prayed that the young poet would continue making spiritual growth.

"Oh good, you found the dinner I left," Jane said, coming into the kitchen with her face flushed. "I went for a long walk. The days are getting hot, aren't they? I've been so busy I hardly noticed."

"Your chicken is delicious," Joanna said. "I'm sorry I missed the dinner. Thank you so much for leaving this for me."

"No problem. I gave most of the baklava to our guests to take home, but I do have a slice left with your name on it."

Alice was proud of her sister for not delving into Joanna's reason for missing dinner. It was up to the poet to explain that she was out seeking food for the soul, not the body.

She suddenly thought of the young woman as a seed blown in the wind, directionless until she found fertile soil in which to blossom.

Was Joanna's poetic nature rubbing off on her? She smiled to herself. She seriously doubted it.

Chapter Ten

When Jane entered the dining room Monday morning, Margo and Ross Wallace were helping themselves to the juice and coffee she'd put on the buffet.

"Good morning," she said cheerfully. "It looks like it will be a wonderful day for bird-watching."

"It will be hard to top yesterday," Ross said. "I was able to check off two species from my list, and we're still puzzling over some musical chirps."

"You are," his wife said with a smile. "I still think it was a house sparrow. I'd know that long monotonous song anywhere."

"She's probably right," her husband admitted. "I like to make a mystery out of sounds I can't identify, but she's the one with the ear for music. She can identify hundreds of birds by their songs."

"Well, not hundreds, but I have been told that I have a sharp ear."

"That's a real gift. I'm nearly totally tone deaf myself. Before I start your breakfast, I wanted to ask if you like avocado," Jane said. "I have an interesting omelet recipe that calls for avocado, but I can substitute something else if you prefer."

"I love avocado," Margo said.

"I'll pass on it," Ross said a bit sheepishly. "A couple of fried eggs would do fine, if you don't mind."

"How about an omelet with sausage and mushrooms?"

"Sounds great."

"Ross is not an adventurous eater, though he certainly is a good eater," his wife teased.

When Jane brought their omelets into the dining room along with a platter of toasted oatmeal-raisin bread, they were quietly reading. Ross was engrossed in studying a map spread out on the table, and Margo was poring over colored illustrations in her bird book.

"If you prefer plain white or whole-wheat toast, I can make some," Jane offered as she put hot plates in front of them."

"This will be lovely," Margo assured her. "Ross has never met a piece of bread he didn't like."

"Do you have a minute?" he asked Jane. "We've been traveling quite a bit. We thought maybe tomorrow we could check out some places in the vicinity. Can you recommend a nice trail near here?"

"Or we could head back to Ohio," Margo quietly suggested.

"Now, Margo, Penny is perfectly fine without us."

"I know," his wife admitted rather sadly. "It's just that we'll see so little of her once school starts."

"We don't see much of her when we're home. That's the way it is when children grow up," he said in a kind voice.

"There is one place near here," Jane tentatively suggested.

"Near town?" Ross asked. "I wouldn't mind not driving at all tomorrow."

"It's called Fairy Lane, and it ends at Fairy Pond. I go that way when I have time for a long walk. The trail starts about a mile north of town off Chapel Road. It's quite pleasant. I would be happy to draw a map for you. I often see birds along the way."

"If there's a pond, there may be nesting water fowl," Margo said.

"Sounds good to me," Ross agreed. "But instead of drawing a map, why don't you join us."

"What a good idea!" his wife agreed.

"I don't know whether I can get away." Their offer was tempting, but she thought of all the things she needed to do in the kitchen.

"We know you love birds," Margo said. "You told us about stocking a winter feeder. That can be quite an obligation once you start."

"It's no bother, really. I'm more than repaid by having feathered neighbors outside my window."

"We understand if you're too busy," Margo said, smiling, "but we'd love your company."

"We wouldn't need to be gone all day," Ross said, apparently not one to give up easily. "We're partial to mornings, but the weather is still cool enough to leave any time during the day."

"Yes, I wouldn't mind having some time to look around in stores here," Margo said. "It takes a lot of shopping to get a daughter ready to leave the nest."

"If I know my wife, Penny will be prepared for anything from tropical heat to arctic cold when she starts college," Ross teased.

"I do tend to overdo," Margo admitted with a grin. "But we really would like to have you join us, Jane."

"Maybe I can get away for a few hours," she said pensively. The prospect of a long walk in the woods was enticing. So was the chance to spend time with bird-watchers who were trained to spot tiny clues that might reveal unusual birds. She believed them when they said there were more than four hundred species in the state, but she'd only seen a tiny fraction of that number.

"Just tell us when you'd like to leave," Margo said.

"I can get away any time after breakfast."

"Be sure to bring binoculars," Margo said.

"Binoculars, yes, good idea." Jane knew that her father had owned a rather good pair. She would have to ask Alice if she knew where they were.

"You'll want a pencil and a notebook too, just a little one that will fit in your pocket." Margo had hardly touched her breakfast, but Ross helped himself to part of her omelet.

"You know, avocado isn't bad," he said after sampling a bite. "When my wife is right, she's right."

"I just enjoy seeing birds," Jane said. "I probably won't bother writing anything about them."

"Trust me, you'll want to keep track of the ones you see. It's so much fun to see your list grow. It's a good way to learn to identify them too. I always travel with my pocket-size bird book so that after we get back to where we're staying, I can read about the ones I've seen that day."

"Bring water too—but you probably know that," Ross said, pushing a few more bites of the avocado omelet onto his plate. "Better eat your breakfast, honey."

"You seem to be doing fine, eating for two," she teased.

"It's a date then," Jane said. "I should be free to leave by nine, if that works for you."

"Great," Ross said, sliding the platter of toast closer to his plate.

"Enough," Margo said, moving it beyond his reach. "We'll have to walk an extra five miles to work off your breakfast. We'll look forward to birding with you, Jane."

Jane was smiling when she walked into the kitchen. There seemed to be a great deal of affection in the couple's teasing. She suspected that she would enjoy an outing with them. In fact, it really was a wonderful opportunity to learn more about bird-watching. There was no downside to a long walk in one of her favorite places.

"You look especially happy this morning," Louise said, as she sat at the table eating her breakfast.

"I'm going bird-watching tomorrow after breakfast with Margo and Ross."

"Good, you need some time off. I'm sorry I won't be here to help."

"It's okay. We're only expecting one guest, a salesman who said that he probably won't get here until tomorrow evening. I'm fixing omelets this morning. How about one with avocado? You need a good breakfast to fortify you for court."

"No, thank you. I'll just have cereal. The county keeps us well fed on jury duty. In fact, perhaps we're too well fed. Most of us are finding that we get sleepy after lunch. I'm going to try a light meal today. I need to keep my head clear. I've heard so much contradictory evidence that it makes my head spin, and I like working with accounts and numbers. I can imagine how confused some jurors must be if they have no bookkeeping experience at all."

"The trial should be over soon, shouldn't it?"

"It's hard to know."

Jane was absolutely sure that Louise was an outstanding juror, as fair and open-minded as anyone could be, but just the same, she would like to have the case wrapped up as soon as possible.

Louise had agreed to drive to Potterston this morning because Florence's car had to go into the shop for servicing.

Florence didn't come out when Louise stopped in front of the Simpsons' spacious older home. Louise waited patiently for a few minutes, then became a bit concerned. Florence didn't make a habit of being late, and certainly she would want to arrive at the courthouse with time to spare. Was it possible she hadn't seen the car pull up? Louise decided to go to the door to see what was keeping her rider.

Ronald answered the door and invited Louise to come inside.

"I just wondered whether Florence is ready to go."

"Should be," her husband said laconically. "Please have a seat in the parlor, and I'll hurry her along."

Louise perched on a balloon-back chair in the elaborately decorated room. The house had been in Florence's family for three generations, and she took great pains to keep the antiques and art objects in an authentic nineteenth-century setting. The deep green curtains were heavy velvet, and the oriental carpet was handwoven, a feast for the eyes in shades of red, green, gold and blue. Florence liked to tell the story of her great-grandfather's buying it on a trip to North Africa.

Unlike the living room at Grace Chapel Inn, this room seemed like a museum. Ronald was never allowed to smoke his signature pipe here for fear of damaging the valuable antiques.

"Louise, I'm so sorry to keep you waiting."

Florence's broad face was flushed, and her plucked and penciled eyebrows were scrunched together in an expression of distress. She'd chosen a very sedate outfit, a plain black suit that could have been called a classic and a tailored white blouse. With sensible black pumps and a tiny hat that was little more than a veil with black-velvet leaves attached to it, she seemed to have dressed for a funeral.

"I had such a nice outfit picked out for today, a plum-colored dress with a silver brooch that used to be my grandmother's. Then I thought the trial might end today. I didn't want to seem frivolous if the case is going to the jury. I mean, we'll have to pick a foreman, and that should be a serious person with leadership qualities. I was ready to go when I decided to change clothes."

Was she going to campaign to be foreman of the jury? Louise smiled to herself. Florence seeking a position in which she could be in charge was really not surprising.

When they got to the courthouse, there was an atmosphere of anticipation in the jury room. The jurors didn't talk about it, but everyone was a bit on edge. Surely today the attorneys would sum up their cases, and the work of the jury would begin.

"If I have to hear another day of lawyers' double-talk while my business goes down the drain, I'll flip," Egbert muttered just before they filed into the court to take their seats in the jury box.

Louise sympathized with him, but she hoped that he would not vote with the majority just to bring in a verdict quickly. Barry Hudson seemed in a particularly bad mood. He complained about the substitute teacher who was taking his chemistry classes and all the end-of-the-year paperwork that he had to catch up on.

"It doesn't seem as if we'll ever get this trial over with," he complained to whoever was within earshot.

Even Eve had lost her enthusiasm for jury duty. Her two small children were taxing her mother-in-law to the maximum, and the whole family was eager to get back to normal.

"Finally," Yvonne whispered to Louise when both sides indicated that they were ready for their summations.

Marlene Gottschek removed her narrow cat's-eyes glasses and let them hang on a chain around her neck when she addressed the jury. She summed up the prosecution's case in a clear, concise way that was very convincing to Louise.

Dick had the responsibility of summing up for the defense. He was certainly the best dressed of the trio, rivaling the defendant's fashion sense in his choice of a beautifully tailored dark blue suit with a white shirt and red tie. His black shoes had been polished until they sparkled, and he'd obviously had his thick mahogany-colored hair styled for the occasion.

Louise noted that Reddenhurst's young wife or perhaps woman friend was again absent. This morning he didn't even look behind him. His face, when he turned it briefly toward the jury, seemed to have aged during the week of the trial. His earlier arrogance had been replaced by resignation. Did he expect to be found guilty? Or was he too upset by personal problems to care about his fate? That was information the jury wouldn't be given, but Louise couldn't help thinking about the possibility.

The defense also did a good job of summarizing its case, but it was hard to concentrate on a repetition of facts they already knew. Louise resisted the urge to shift her weight in the chair, but she was aware of other jurors fidgeting and shuffling their feet. Beside her, Yvonne crossed and uncrossed her legs so frequently that Louise wanted to tell her to sit still.

By lunchtime it was over. The judge gave the jurors instructions, and it was up to them to make a decision.

Instead of trooping over to the restaurant, they had a catered lunch brought to the jury room. It was a nice cold buffet, but Louise had no appetite. A couple of the men loaded their plates, but most of the others seemed as eager as she was to get on with the business that had brought them together.

As he had throughout the trial, Mr. Otto was there to instruct them on procedure. In Louise's opinion, the bailiff was the unsung hero of the court system. He had to be a person with immense patience to go through trial after trial, shepherding untrained jurors through their responsibilities, alert for any misconduct or lapses. She wasn't at all sure what the jury should do now, but he was quick to explain.

"You have to choose a foreman," he said.

"Well, who wants the job?" Egbert said in a tone that made it clear that he didn't.

People looked at each other, no one quite willing to volunteer. Louise turned her attention to Florence, who did want the job. Should she suggest her neighbor? She hesitated, not sure that Florence would be the right person for the job.

Florence took a deep breath, as though she were about to volunteer for an unpleasant task, but before she could say a word, Bertha Haywood spoke up. "I think Louise would be a fine choice," Bertha said. "She gets along with everyone, and she has such good sense."

Louise was surprised. Bertha had been a rather inattentive juror, pleasant but not very talkative. She was in her sixties and worked for the county road commission. She waged a daily battle not to fall asleep in the courtroom after lunch. In fact, she'd enlisted Ella Girard to nudge her if her head nodded during testimony.

"I'll go along with that," the chemistry teacher said, another surprising development since he hadn't exchanged ten words with her in the course of the trial. "I've noticed that whenever there has been discussion, you seem to make intelligent suggestions, Louise."

"I agree," several others said.

"Thank you, all, but isn't anyone else interested in being foreperson?" Louise asked.

She didn't feel that she should refuse if the rest really wanted her, but she sensed Florence's disappointment. Louise felt an obligation to at least mention her name, suspecting that Florence would be quite hurt if she didn't.

"Florence is well-qualified for the job," she continued. "She heads up quite a few organizations."

No one paid any attention. Sterling and Everett both called for a show of hands, and Louise found herself elected foreperson of the jury.

Mr. Otto provided further information about procedures and then allowed the jury to get down to business.

"Now can we take a vote about this case?" Egbert asked.

"He's guilty. Let's get this over with," Yvonne said. "I'm missing sales every day I'm cooped up here. This is the prime season for home buying."

"Shouldn't we talk it over first?" Sterling asked. The quiet middle-aged accountant liked to weigh everything that was said to him, and he clearly didn't want to rush an important decision like the one facing them.

"I think it would be in order if we review the evidence on both sides first, then go around the table and let everyone express his or her opinion before taking a formal vote," Louise said, hoping that she was following the right procedure.

"That will take all day," Egbert protested.

"This is a very serious situation. A man's future is in our hands," Sterling said.

"Please, we've been lectured enough by the judge. Let's get on with it," Yvonne insisted.

Even though it was somewhat tedious, they went over the main points in the case. Louise encouraged the other jurors to ask questions about any facet of the case that they didn't understand. Finally it was time to find out how everyone stood.

"Would you like to start?" Louise asked Egbert, who as yet hadn't given any clues about how he might vote. "Let's talk about the charge of embezzling from the Reddenhurst department store first."

"Well, it's his company, isn't it?" Egbert said.

"Was," Yvonne broke in. "He didn't have any right to claim expense money for all those fancy vacations he took."

"The defense argued that he was owed back salary for serving on the board of directors," Mona the bank teller reminded them.

When several jurors started talking at the same time, Louise realized her job as foreperson wasn't going to be easy. She tapped on the table with the end of a pen and called for quiet.

"We'll waste a lot of time if everyone tries to talk at once. Now, let's continue to go around the table in order. When each of us has had his say, we'll take an initial vote just to see where we stand. Remember, we have to have a unanimous decision. That means listening to arguments on both sides and having respect for other people's opinions. Is there anything else you want to say, Egbert?"

"I guess not. I haven't made up my mind yet." He sounded reluctant to admit it.

"Yvonne, you're next. Would you like to give your reasons for thinking Mr. Reddenhurst is guilty of embezzling from the store?"

"He stole money that was supposed to go to charities."

"We'll get to that. Right now we're talking about the first charge, embezzling from the store."

Louise sighed to herself. An already long day was beginning to seem endless.

Alice was happy to be back at work after her two-week break, but she found herself thinking about Cynthia's friend as she went about her duties.

Alice knew that Joanna was excited about sharing her interests with children, and it really was good to have an adult help with the program. The ANGEL who had been scheduled to read was tied up with choir practice, so there was a perfect opening for Joanna to fill.

The children would be dropped off at the library by four o'clock, which gave Alice just enough time to get to the library before the program began.

As she drove toward Acorn Hill after work, Alice wondered what Joanna planned to read. Fortunately, Nia would check on that. The children were young, ages five and six, and it was important that they hear something age-appropriate.

When she got inside the library, she was pleased with the arrangements that had been made. Tables in the children's area had been arranged in a long line and covered with old newspaper, so they wouldn't be marked up by felt pens. Even though Nia was sure to have chosen pens with washable ink, it would be much easier to strip off the paper than to scrub all the tabletops.

She saw that Joanna was there ahead of her, busily arranging the child-size chairs in a circle. That was good. The kiddies would listen better if they were gathered around her. They could go to the tables later for refreshments and their crafts.

"Is everything ready?" she asked the two women.

"So it seems," Nia said, a quick smile wiping away a frown.

Was the librarian worried about the project? Alice got the feeling that she and Joanna had disagreed on something.

"What can I do to help?" she asked, directing her question at Joanna, who was busy assembling cardboard boxes that she must have gotten from the grocery store.

"Oh, nothing, thanks. I'm almost done."

"What are the boxes for?" Alice watched as she put them in stacks beside the tables. There was one for each child.

"You'll see," Joanna said happily.

She'd dressed in a long flowered skirt with a mint green top that matched the background color. It was flattering to her reddish-blond hair, and she seemed unusually animated as she scurried around the table, her yellow flip-flops slapping softly against her bare heels. In fact, she looked prettier than she had at any time since arriving in Acorn Hill. She was obviously enjoying herself.

Alice was nervous as the children started to arrive. Fifteen children had signed up, and she very much regretted that none of her ANGELs were there to give individual attention. The girls tied up by the choir practice had tried to find substitutes, but it was a busy time of year, especially for those involved in spring sports. The conflict between the library project and the concert rehearsals couldn't be helped. Luckily, the ANGELs would be there in force to continue the program the next week.

The children were excited and a bit unruly at first, but they settled down nicely when Joanna clapped her hands and told them she had a story to share with them. She told it quite dramatically without reading from a book, acting out the parts and drawing the children into it by asking them to participate in small ways. Joanna proved to be a master storyteller and did a wonderful job in pleasing the children with an unexpected ending. "I can't remember hearing that story before," Alice whispered to the librarian.

"She wrote it herself. I was a bit worried, but she seems to know how to interest children," Nia whispered back. "Now if the crafts go well, we'll be off to a fine start."

They served refreshments first, fifteen cups of fruit juice, and graham cracker sandwiches with peanut butter filling. Only one girl spilled her drink, and it soaked harmlessly into the paper that covered the table.

"Now we'll really have some fun," Joanna said when the cups and crumbs had been cleared. "We're going to make pantins."

She said it with the enthusiasm of a circus ringmaster, but it was obvious that the children didn't have a clue what she meant.

"How many of you like to play with paper dolls?"

Several girls raised their hands, but two of the boys snickered at each other and tilted their chairs back on two legs. It took a moment for Nia to convince them to keep all four legs on the floor.

"Paper dolls are for girls," said one boy with a buzz cut and a garishly decorated black T-shirt.

"Oh, you think so, do you? Well, pantins are much more than paper dolls. They're paper puppets, and, as you know, puppeteers are both male and female. The boxes in front of you are theaters," Joanna said.

She momentarily stifled her critic as she began pulling out stacks of things from her big tote.

"Pantin is a French word for puppet," Joanna explained. "Adults liked to play with them more than two hundred and fifty years ago. Each of you will make a paper puppet, and I'll show you how to get it to dance so it'll seem sort of real. I'll pass out all the things you will need."

Now Alice knew how Joanna had spent her day. She'd cut the bodies and heads from poster board and punched holes to attach legs and arms with pieces of string. Another hole in the top of each head would allow the children to dance the puppets on a cord. Joanna had also shaped one side of each box to form an opening for the stage and cut a hole in the top for the string that would control the puppet. The preparation had involved a lot of work—and a lot of time not spent on her editing.

"First we'll decorate them. Pass around these felt pens and take a couple of your favorite colors. I brought lots of paper to make clothes, or you can draw your own. Here's yarn for hair, string to tie on the legs and arms—not too tightly because you want them to dance. There's enough glue and scissors for everyone."

"I don't want to make a paper doll." Randy folded his arms across his chest in a posture of resistance.

"Me neither," said his buddy.

"I only got yellow and purple. I wanted red," a little girl at the end of the table complained.

"We'll all share," Joanna patiently assured her.

"I don't know how to tie." A small boy with large blue eyes and wildly rumpled brown hair said.

"I'll help you."

"My fingers are sticky. I need to wash my hands," a dark-haired girl in jeans and a yellow T-shirt said. She'd managed to squeeze out a big dollop of glue and smear it around in front of her.

"I need to wash my hands too," the girl next to her said.

Joanna was explaining the difference between the arms and the legs that she'd cut, hoping the children would distinguish between right and left limbs.

A third girl expressed an urgent need to wash a smear of green from her fingers.

Alice shepherded the three girls to the restroom, waiting calmly while they enjoyed squirting pink soap on their hands. One of them came up and whispered confidentially, "I don't want to make one of those things. I want to make a kitty."

"I'd like to make a kitty too," chimed in another child.

"Let's give the pantins—the puppets—a try," Alice said sympathetically. "It will be fun to glue on the hair. What color yarn do you like best?"

"Purple."

"You can't have purple hair," her friend said.

"Yes, I can. My aunt has blue hair."

Alice choked back a laugh and tried to squelch the debate about hair color as she ushered them back to the craft table. The situation had not improved in her absence.

"I want another one. This one is no good," one boy was saying, aggressively waving a hideously colored head and torso at Joanna.

Nia was helping tie arms and legs, getting her hands dyed by the ink from the felt pens in the process. Randy was making spit balls from the colored paper that was supposed to be used for his puppet's clothing. Alice put a stop to his bombardment, but not before he'd hit an indignant girl wearing pink-framed glasses.

"My hands are sticky," a strident voice called out.

Alice caught a glimpse of a girl energetically wiping white glue on a pretty purple top. One of the boys was tattooing his arm with a green felt pen. She didn't want to guess what the bizarre object on his pale forearm was supposed to be.

"You're not supposed to draw on yourself," a rather self-righteous girl beside him said.

"These scissors don't work," another voice complained.

"They're fine for paper. You're not supposed to cut the cardboard," Joanna said, her voice sounding ragged. "Now, who needs help tying on arms and legs?"

Alice exchanged a look with Nia, fighting an urge to apologize for letting Joanna loose in the library.

One of the boys actually finished his pantin, making it bob up and down at a frenetic pace.

"Let me see that." Randy's friend grabbed it away, ripping off one arm in the process.

"He broke my thing."

"I'll help you fix it," Alice said, stepping into the fray. She rescued the pantin, and Nia went to find tape to repair it.

Alice walked the offender to a table in the adult reading area and told him to sit there quietly until it was time to go home. He protested, but she was firm. Unfortunately, the next time she looked in his direction, he was removing magazines from the racks, stacking them up in front of him.

Nia started to say something about calling his parents, but she was distracted by a boy who was pooling the white glue in a puddle in front of him. "What are you doing?"

"This glue doesn't come out good. I need a lot for the hair."

"My hair keeps coming off," another complained.

"My puppet is bald like my uncle," one of the handwashers said. "He shaves his head so people won't know that he doesn't have enough to cover his plate."

"I don't think you mean 'plate,'" Joanna said before she was distracted by a boy who was standing on his box. "What are you doing?"

"I want to squash it down. That's how my mom recycles boxes. They won't take them unless they're flat."

"You're supposed to make a theater, not recycle it."

Joanna sounded close to tears. Obviously she'd never worked with young children. Her idea was splendid, but not for the age of these youngsters. Alice only hoped that the children would want to give the program another try. If all of them dropped out, her ANGELs would be terribly disappointed.

"Okay, it's time to play a game," she said, frantically trying to remember something that might appeal to all of them.

"We'll play indoor baseball."

"The girls against the boys," someone called out.

"Fine."

Nia helped her arrange chairs for the bases and took a turn as the pitcher, asking questions of the batters to advance them to first base or strike them out. They tried to make the questions somewhat humorous and easy enough that most of the children could answer. It wasn't the kind of baseball some of the boys might have favored, but it filled the time until parents started coming to collect their boys and girls.

No one took a theater box home, and all but a few of the haphazardly completed pantins were left behind on the table. When everyone had left, Alice helped Nia and Joanna clean up.

"It was a very nice story. Thank you for all you did," Nia said to Joanna when they were ready to leave. "Maybe the craft would have worked better with older children."

Joanna sat beside Alice in her car, which she hadn't had time to drop off at the inn before the session with the children began.

"Maybe I'll forget about finger painting tomorrow. We could play a game on the front lawn," she said.

"I think that's a good decision," Alice said, surprised that Joanna fully intended to continue working in the program.

At home, Joanna went up to her room while Alice went into the kitchen, where she found both of her sisters at the table. When they looked up at her questioningly, she said, "Don't ask!" and slumped, exhausted, into a chair.

Chapter Eleven

"A letter for me might come to the inn," Joanna said Tuesday morning as she toyed with a serving of Jane's egg and sausage casserole.

"I'll be sure to give it to you if one arrives," Jane told her. "If you don't mind, I'll start clearing the table now. I'm going bird-watching with the Wallaces. You don't need to hurry, though. Take as long as you like to finish."

"Has Alice left for work?" Joanna asked. "I wanted to talk to her about the library program."

"Yes, she ate with Louise and left shortly afterward."

"The three of you certainly keep busy, don't you? I can't thank you enough for letting me stay here with Cynthia."

"Did I hear my name?"

Cynthia walked into the kitchen dressed for work in slender-legged khaki trousers and a sleeveless orange knit top with a multicolored cotton scarf tied at the neck. Jane admired the way her niece made even a casual outfit look stylish.

"I was just thanking Jane for letting me stay here with you," Joanna explained.

"Yes, it has been a real joy to be able to come here, Aunt Jane," Cynthia said, giving her aunt a hug. Then she turned to Joanna.

"We need to have a serious conversation when you finish breakfast."

"Oh dear, am I in trouble? I know I was a few days late in mailing the revisions to the author, but she promised to get right at them. There were some tricky parts that just didn't gel for me."

"When did you send them to her?"

"Let's see, today is Tuesday. I think it was early yesterday morning, before I went shopping for the craft project at the library."

"You should have shown your revision memo to me first. In any case, you were so late that she won't have enough time to make the revisions before the deadline. You can't expect an author to complete revisions in only a few days," Cynthia said in a weary voice.

"Excuse me for interrupting," Jane said, "but I have to get ready to go. Cynthia, there's some breakfast casserole left in the oven. I would appreciate it if you put whatever you don't eat into the fridge. Have a nice day, you two."

"I'll take care of it, Aunt Jane. Have fun bird-watching."

As Jane left the kitchen, she heard Cynthia pick up the discussion with Joanna, her voice solemn.

Alice was only scheduled to work half a shift that day, so she arrived home before lunch. She found Joanna in the kitchen, sweeping the black-and-white tiled floor, scattering more crumbs than she gathered.

"Alice, I wanted to help out, but I'm glad you're back," she said, abandoning the broom in the center of the room. "I need to talk to you."

Joanna sat on a chair and puckered her brow in thought. "I've been thinking about the library," she said.

"If it's interfering with your work, don't feel that you have to continue. I happened to see Nia as I was driving into town. I stopped and chatted for a few minutes. She loved the way you read to the children, but she thought perhaps you need more help during the crafts-and-games part of the program. My ANGELs can't begin helping until next week, so she asked several of the children's mothers to help. They were delighted to be involved."

"You mean I've been fired?" Joanna looked close to tears.

"Goodness, no. You're the official reader. Just let Nia know what you've chosen, and she'll let you handle the story hour. She did suggest that you come in ahead of time and look over a few of the new books she's putting out. The object of the program is to acquaint children with the books that the library has to offer."

"I guess I shouldn't have told a story I made up."

"It was a nice story, only Nia wants to call attention to books in the library's circulating collection."

"I can do that. I'll run over to the library as soon as I can and select a book for today." She glanced at the doorway where Cynthia had left.

"Run along then. That's a good idea to stop by the library, but I don't want to keep you from your job. That has to come first."

Joanna rose reluctantly from her chair and moved slowly out

of the kitchen. Alice plopped down at the table feeling as though all the air had rushed out of her lungs. Working with Joanna was complicated. Sometimes she was overly sensitive, but she also could be oblivious to what was required of her. On the other hand, she could be completely dedicated to the things that interested her. She had a unique slant on life, but she wasn't always able to see things from other people's perspectives. Alice felt sad for her. Joanna had tremendous potential. She was very bright and energetic, but her personality quirks tended to keep her from accomplishing her goals.

Louise was willing to hear Florence's ideas as they drove to Potterston, but she wasn't at all sure that she agreed with her take on the jury situation.

"As I see it, you should make Yvonne be quiet. She's already made up her mind, and she only irritates the rest of the jury. Goodness, I think she would vote to hang Reddenhurst if she could. I'm tired of her ranting," Florence said dismissively.

Louise wasn't happy with the anger and the negative attitude that the Realtor brought to the jury, but she knew that each member had to be given time to express his or her feelings about the case.

"Of course, I'm not the foreperson," Florence said, making a valiant effort to be a good sport about it, "but if I were, I would worry about Sterling Hagar. He can't even decide what to have for lunch. It could take weeks for him to make up his mind."

"We don't know that," Louise said mildly.

Her lack of agreement didn't discourage Florence.

"Everett Eskridge is another one of those quiet types, hard to read. He has a home business, so he isn't used to working with other people."

"He's a pleasant man," Louise said, trying to think of a topic of conversation that wouldn't involve Florence's opinions about the jurors. "By the way, I'm hoping to get home as early as possible today. Cynthia is still visiting, you know. Do you have any errands that have to be done on the way?"

"Well, I was hoping to drop Ronald's slacks at the tailor shop, but if you need to get home, I can postpone it until the next time I drive."

"Thank you. I would appreciate that."

"I am so tired of hearing about Mr. Denison's garden," Florence continued. "All he talks about is his little village. I think he would rather lord it over his miniature village than deal with the real world."

It made Louise uncomfortable to analyze the other members of the jury. They weren't the ones on trial. "A hobby is good when you're retired." Louise tried again to distract her. "Is Ronald going to be chairman of the building and grounds committee at the chapel for another year? He did such a nice job organizing cleanup day."

"Probably." Ronald's volunteer work wasn't what Florence wanted to discuss. "I'm so grateful that I'm more alert than Mrs. Haywood. She's not even as old as I am, but every time I glance over at her, her lids are drooping. She would have fallen asleep in court if Ella Girard hadn't been there to nudge her from time to time. Really, she should know enough to go to bed early so she can stay awake during the day."

Louise was as concerned as Florence about how the personalities of the jury would affect their decisions, but the last thing she wanted was to hear gossip. Unfortunately, Florence was unstoppable.

"Judge Findlay scares me just a tiny bit. He reminds me of my grandfather. Granddad had a way of looking at me when I was naughty that made me feel like crying. It was as though I'd disappointed him, and he didn't expect that kind of behavior from me. Of course, I was always a very obedient child, so that didn't happen often. Anyway, I would hate to go back into that courtroom and tell the judge that we can't reach a decision. If I were the foreperson, I would make sure that didn't happen."

Louise was beginning to wish that Florence were the foreperson.

The drive to Potterston seemed doubly long this morning, and Louise was drained from her conversation with Florence.

"Go ahead. I'll be right with you," Louise said when they parked in the lot near the courthouse. She didn't even try to explain that she needed a few moments alone.

Florence, of course, wanted an explanation, but when Louise didn't offer one, she reluctantly set off for the courthouse on her own.

"Dear Lord," Louise said in a whispered prayer, "please give me the strength to get through this and the wisdom to see that we make a just decision."

She was one of the last to arrive in the jury room. Mr. Otto had arranged for coffee and sweet rolls, and most of the jurors were helping themselves.

"Can't complain that the county hasn't kept us fed," Lee Denison said, piling a Danish and two doughnuts on a small paper plate.

"If everyone has coffee, let's sit down and begin," Louise said.

"Can't we take a vote and get this over with?" Yvonne said.

Mona and Eve were chatting with each other by the window, ignoring Louise's request to begin deliberations.

"If you wouldn't mind joining us," Louise said.

"My time is money," the lawn man said belligerently. "I can't sit around here all day while my brother-in-law runs my business into the ground."

The two women seemed to delay deliberately after Egbert's comment, and Louise had to ask them again, this time more firmly. Finally everyone was seated at the table. It was interesting that each person went to exactly the same chair every time, almost as though they had assigned seats. Louise wondered if that signified something.

"So, are we going to vote?" Egbert asked.

"I want a secret ballot," Barry Hudson said. "That way no one will feel pressured to go along with anyone else's vote."

"We can do it that way," Louise agreed. "But remember, we have to decide separately on the store and on the foundation charges."

"Shouldn't we have two separate ballots then?" Florence asked.

"Yes, let's do that," Eve said. "I feel surer about one than the other."

Louise agreed, even though the process of taking two separate votes took far longer than it should have. Some of the jurors couldn't resist commenting as they voted, and there was a minor dispute over who would tally them. Louise asked Sterling Hagar. She expected him to be the most businesslike, but he turned out to be painfully slow, smoothing and piling up the slips of paper as though they were precious documents.

The results made her heart sink. There were seven guilty votes for each count. They had a long way to go. Louise thought of what Florence had said about Judge Findlay and realized that she, too, would hate going back into the courtroom without reaching a unanimous decision.

While moderating the point-by-point discussion, Louise got a pretty good idea of where most of the jurors stood. Eve, Mona, Doris, Barry, Lee and Florence stood firm on thinking Reddenhurst was guilty. Louise had voted with them, although her thinking wasn't as inflexible as theirs. Egbert surprised her. He didn't say much other than to complain about having to be there, so she wasn't sure why he thought Reddenhurst was innocent. Sterling and Everett were more inclined to talk to each other than the group, but she gathered that neither thought the prosecutor had made a good case for a guilty verdict. Bertha Haywood was rather inattentive, even in the jury room, so her reasoning was also a mystery.

Ella Girard was the hardest of all to read. She was a worrier, stewing over everything from the possibility of rain to the danger of using an artificial sweetener in her coffee. Louise knew from fragments of conversation that she didn't have a very happy life.

Money was very tight, and she didn't get any emotional support from her husband, who preferred to spend his leisure time with his buddies. She was not at all forthcoming on her reasons for thinking Reddenhurst was innocent.

After a long morning of debate, the talk sometimes going in circles without resulting in any real progress, they stopped for a catered lunch. Louise's mind was racing as she picked at her food, wondering how they would ever come to a decision.

Jane went through her lightweight denim backpack one more time to make sure she had everything. She'd made up three bags of trail mix. Her mix was a bit more exotic than the usual packaged variety. Instead of peanuts, she used macadamia nuts and cashews. Dates and dried pineapple were substituted for the raisins, and she added crunch to the mix with banana chips, sunflower seeds and miniature pretzels.

She packed an ample supply of water, a notebook and pencil, a purse-size packet of tissues, some handwipes, sunscreen, insect repellent, sunglasses and, of course, a cap with a bill. She smiled at the array of equipment for a trip so close to home, but she was experienced enough to know that walking was more fun without sunburn, itchy bites, an empty stomach and dehydration.

Fortunately, she'd found her father's binoculars, and she added a small camera to her pack. She might not capture many birds on film, but some shots of Fairy Pond and the woods might inspire her the next time she wanted to do some painting.

"I'm ready," she said as she met Margo and Ross in the front hall. Like Jane, they'd opted for trousers and long-sleeved shirts as protection from branches, brambles and bugs.

Jane was excited about the prospect of seeing unusual birds, and Ross seemed to share her enthusiasm. Margo was very quiet, but Jane hoped she would perk up once they were on the lovely winding trail.

"You're the leader," Ross said. "This is your neck of the woods."

"We could walk from here, but it will add a couple of miles to our hike. If you like, we could drive and park the car in a lay-by near the beginning of the trail."

"That sounds good, doesn't it?" he asked his wife.

"Yes, fine."

"I might as well drive then," Ross said.

They went to the dark red SUV parked on the street, and Ross loaded their backpacks in the rear. Margo insisted Jane ride in front with her husband.

"There's not as much leg room in back, and I'm a lot shorter than you are."

It was the last thing she said until they parked the vehicle and were on their way into the woods. Jane was sorry that Margo didn't seem to be enjoying her vacation as much as she would have if their daughter had come, but Jane decided not to let the woman's somber mood spoil the day.

The trail to Fairy Pond was a little-known treasure. It penetrated an old-growth forest of pine and hemlock trees that had sprouted before William Penn gave his name to the new colony of Pennsylvania. Somehow the forest had escaped demolition by logging crews and destruction by fire, storms or tornadoes.

Jane felt privileged to walk through the towering trees. She saw the forest as a great natural cathedral, in some ways a more fitting place of worship than anything man could build. A feeling of reverence came over her, and her companions seemed to share it. All of them spoke in hushed voices, and for a while Jane forgot that they were there to spot birds.

Margo's mood seemed to lighten as they proceeded into the forest. She was the first to spot a flash of scarlet deeper in the woods, which Ross was quick to call a summer tanager.

"No, I think it was a scarlet tanager," his wife said.

They debated in a friendly way for several minutes until Ross was persuaded.

"She's got the best eye and ear in our bird-watching club," he said with pride. "Give her a feather, and she'll tell you the name of the bird."

"I'm not that good," Margo protested, although she was obviously pleased by his compliment.

"She can hear just a few notes and identify the bird," he continued.

"Well, it didn't take much skill to identify the source of our serenade last night," she said, laughing.

"There was a bird outside your window?" Jane asked.

"Oh yes, and he had quite a repertoire," Ross said.

"It was a northern mockingbird," Margo explained. "You know, the males may sing all night when there's a full moon in spring or summer."

"Oh dear, I hope you got some sleep," Jane said.

"Don't worry, for us it was a lovely lullaby," Margo said, then pointed up and ahead of them. "Look, a hooded warbler."

By the time Jane had adjusted her binoculars and managed to focus on the place where the bird had been, it had gone. There obviously was more to bird-watching than just waiting to see them. She had to admire Margo's keen eye and quick reaction.

What she missed on the wing, Jane made up for on the ground. She soon found herself checking both sides of the trail for spots of color that indicated wildflowers in bloom. She was rewarded when she found some little pink flowers at the base of an evergreen tree.

"Look, trailing arbutus," Margo said excitedly.

"There's a bird I've never heard of," Ross teased.

"It's a wildflower, silly," his wife said, leaning close to the plant without touching it.

Jane snapped a picture, hoping it would turn out well despite the dappled light. A small grouping of wildflower pictures would be lovely in the upper hallway where she and her sisters had their rooms.

Ross and Margo both pointed out birds as they spotted them, but Jane had to admit that most of the time she only saw a bare branch or, at best, a flash of tail feathers. But she didn't miss any opportunities to photograph wildflowers.

"Look, a jack-in-the-pulpit," she said, pointing at a purplish flower with fleshy red fruits. "I almost never see those."

Her day seemed complete when she got a glimpse of wild ginger, a creeping plant with little bell-shaped flowers that grew near the ground between heart- and kidney-shaped leaves. She couldn't resist snapping more pictures.

Margo and Ross went a bit ahead of her, excited by a birdcall Margo was trying to identify. Jane was more excited about the plants on the forest floor because they didn't fly away before she could spot them. Of course, it was strictly forbidden to disturb them, but she wished that she could transplant some of the wildflowers to her own garden.

"Jane, come hear this," Margo called back to her.

She listened to the little chirp, but it sounded much like any other birdcall to her.

"I don't have my sister's ear for music," she admitted when Margo's efforts to explain the notes failed.

Jane got a bit ahead of the Wallaces when they went a few paces off the trail trying to spot the nest of an elusive Kentucky warbler. She was distracted by a little gasp from Margo.

"What's wrong?" she asked, turning toward the couple.

"We've found a fledgling," Margo said.

"When babies are still in the nest, they're called nestlings," Ross explained. "It's a natural thing for the babies to leave the nest even before they can fly."

"The nest becomes too crowded," Margo said, bending over for a better look at the featherless little creature.

"Will it survive?" Jane asked with a worried frown.

"It has a good chance if it can get to a more sheltered place. I'm going to scoop it up and carry it over to those bushes," she said.

"I thought the mother bird would reject her babies if a human handled them or the nest," Jane said.

"Not at all," Ross said. "Birds have a weak sense of smell, but they will hear the baby's chirps and bring it food. They'll continue to take care of their offspring until they can fend for themselves. The only danger in touching a bird's nest is leaving a human scent on it that predators can follow."

Jane watched with awe as Margo very carefully scooped the tiny baby bird into her gloved hand, taking care not to let it struggle and hurt itself. When she'd deposited it in covering vegetation, it was invisible.

"That should do it," she said with a broad smile. "With any luck, it'll be fine. The parents won't abandon it if it's strong enough to chirp and get their attention."

Jane was delighted that Margo had been able to help the tiny creature survive.

"Let's go on to the pond," her husband said.

"Yes, let's. I'm eager to see if we spot any nesting waterbirds," Margo agreed cheerfully.

Fairy Pond was as beautiful as Jane remembered, although the ground around it was too soggy from spring rains to allow them to get close. They saw a few birds on the wing, but the experienced bird-watchers weren't able to spot any nests.

"We would need hip waders to get close enough," Ross said.

"It's just as well that we don't disturb any nesters," Margo said. "Preserving wildlife is just as important to us as seeing it.

We haven't seen as many species as I'd hoped. You're not disappointed, Jane, are you?"

"Anything but!" she said emphatically.

"You took quite a few photos," Ross said.

"Yes, I loved seeing the wildflowers," Jane said. "It seems I'm better at spotting things on the ground than in the treetops," she said, laughing. "Maybe that's why I can easily spot robins when they come back in the spring. They're always in my garden trying to get those juicy worms."

"I hate to burst your bubble, Jane," Ross said, "but those same robins were probably in the woods all winter long. It's a bit of a myth that they go south for the winter and return in the spring."

"Really? I never heard that before," Jane said.

"Yes," Margo put in. "They're called facultative migrants, meaning they migrate only when the berries and fruit that they eat in the winter aren't available, say, because of an ice storm. Then they go only as far south as they must to find food."

"You mean if it's a mild winter, they're here all the time?"

"That's right," Margo said. "They come out of the woods and into the open when spring comes because then they can get their warm-weather food like worms, caterpillars and grubs."

"I feel ashamed that I don't even know something important like that about robins," Jane admitted.

Ross laughed. "You'd be surprised at the amount of misinformation there is about birds. Another example is the belief that when birds eat the rice thrown at weddings it swells in their stomachs and kills them. Birds can and do eat rice from rice fields with no problem. That's the same as the rice we find at the market."

"Oh my, wait until I tell my aunt Ethel. She insisted that the church's wedding committee refuse to let rice be thrown because of that myth. Only birdseed is permitted."

"Well, I must say I like the idea of throwing birdseed instead," Margo said. "So maybe it's just as well to let her continue to believe the myth."

"Yes, perhaps I will. That will make for a happier aunt and happier birds."

Chapter Twelve 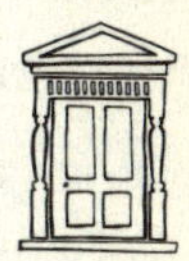

"How did things go at the library yesterday?" Louise asked when she and Jane joined Alice for a very early breakfast Wednesday before she had to go to work. "I've been so wrapped up in the trial that I feel out of touch."

"A couple of the mothers did the crafts and led the children in a game, but Joanna read the story. It was quite a long one and perhaps a little beyond the younger children, but all in all, things went better than on Monday," Alice said.

"I'm happy to hear that, both for you and for Joanna," Louise said. "Now, I'm afraid I have to do a few things before I'm ready to go."

"Do you think this will be your last day?" Jane asked.

"I'm not optimistic about that. It's almost as if some of the jurors want to drag this out. Maybe they like the change in the normal pace of their days or even the nice lunches. It's really hard on those of us who are eager to finish. If the bailiff, Mr. Otto, is to be believed, the judge is getting a bit cross at the delay."

"What happens if the jury can't agree?" Alice asked, standing to leave.

"It will be declared a mistrial, and that's not good. Imagine having to do the whole thing over again. It's not as if the prosecutor and judge don't have other cases to pursue."

"Maybe they'll let the defendant plead guilty to a lesser charge," Alice suggested. "I've heard that happens a lot."

"Possibly," Louise said thoughtfully, "but is that really justice? If he's innocent, he shouldn't be scared into plea bargaining. If he's guilty, it doesn't seem fair to let him off without a penalty that fits his crime, the same that would be given to a person who couldn't afford to pay for high-powered attorneys."

"Imagine how much his defense lawyers are costing," Jane said. "I wonder why the defendant thought he needed three of them in court with him."

Louise shrugged. Aside from differences in appearance, the trio had pretty much spoken as one voice in arguing for their client.

After her sisters had left, Jane prepared breakfast for Cynthia and Joanna, a simple task since her niece only wanted a bowl of cereal and Joanna was satisfied with juice and toast.

Both young women talked to her, but they didn't say much to each other. Jane suspected that the tension between them had to do with work, so she elected to escape into the pantry to straighten some shelves and give them time to discuss their problems.

She could hear Cynthia's voice, calm and reasonable, discussing the younger woman's editing project.

"No one told me that I had to go through you on this," Joanna responded defensively. "I thought it was my project."

"It is," Cynthia agreed. "But there are a few problems, and I thought I could help you with them."

"Well, it's too late. I think I did a good job cleaning up a bad manuscript. It wasn't my decision to buy it, you know."

"Of course, but the staff tries to work as a team. I hope you'll be a member of it for a long time to come. Well, what's done is done. Let's go into the library and sort through the slush pile for something you'd like to read."

The women left the kitchen, and Jane emerged from the pantry. She admired her niece's patience and tact. Even as a little girl, she had been careful of other people's feelings, and her natural skills were serving her well as an adult. Jane suspected that Joanna's editing would not pass muster, but certainly Cynthia had done all she could to help her, including bringing her to Grace Chapel Inn.

After her pleasant outing the day before, Jane wanted to make up for her time away from the inn by accomplishing a lot today. She wiped out the oven and set it to clean. Then she turned her attention to her large assortment of spices. It had been too long since she'd updated them.

A couple of times a year she liked to go through her extensive collection and restock any that were low or had passed their freshness date. She started checking and soon found that the coriander was nearly gone. She had quite a few recipes that used the spice, so it was the first one she wrote on her shopping list.

Sage she jotted down next. Besides its traditional use in stuffing, she occasionally used it in salads, omelets, bread and even tomato juice.

She bought cinnamon in large tin containers, so there was

still an adequate supply. The dill was low, though. She used it regularly with fish, soup and potatoes.

How long had it been since she'd replaced the basil? She checked the "best by" date on the bottom of the jar and saw that it was months past that date. The leaves did look rather anemic. To deliver their sweet, warm flavor they had to be robustly green.

The container of parsley was almost new. She only used it when fresh parsley wasn't on hand. The oregano was also recently purchased. She couldn't imagine making a pizza without it, and it was important in a number of recipes. She shook a little tin of saffron, wondering if it would suffice for a while longer. It was wonderful for adding a touch of color, and the aromatic, slightly bitter spice was a necessary addition to certain recipes. Still, it was very expensive, so she decided not to buy more now.

Her spices were arranged alphabetically, a system that took a little extra work to maintain but saved time when she was cooking. She liked to know exactly what she had and be able to put her hand on it immediately. She'd known a few chefs who were messy and disorganized, and they caused a lot of grief for those who had to work with them.

"Good morning!" a familiar voice trilled from the doorway.

Ethel came into the kitchen looking particularly chipper in a yellow print dress with little red hummingbirds and purple trumpet-shaped flowers.

"Aunt Ethel, come have a cup of tea with me. What are you up to this morning?"

"Oh, I have errands," she said. "Return a library book, visit the pharmacy."

"Would you like to try a new flavor of tea this morning? I have an interesting new assortment of tea bags."

"So often they don't taste anything like their name," she said a bit dubiously. "What do you suggest?"

"How about coffee mocha?"

"Coffee-flavored tea? That doesn't make much sense to me. If someone wanted that flavor, why not just drink coffee?"

"How about almond spice or raspberry?" Jane said, consulting the choices she had left.

"Fruit flavors are especially disappointing, I've found. I'll try almond spice, please."

Jane had made the tea and sat down to visit with her aunt when Ross Wallace came to the kitchen door.

"I know I'm late," he said apologetically, "but is there any chance I can get a cup of coffee?"

"Of course," Jane said with a smile. "Come join us. This is my aunt, Ethel Buckley. She lives in the carriage house. Aunt Ethel, this is our guest, Ross Wallace. He and his wife are using the inn as a base for their bird-watching holiday. They were nice enough to take me along yesterday."

The large, sandy-haired man sat down beside Ethel. He dwarfed her in size, making her look like a pixie. She immediately engaged him in conversation, loving to find out all she could about any newcomer.

"Where are you from?" she asked.

"Ohio, a little town outside Cleveland called Berrien Hills."

"Is there much work in your town? I was a farm wife myself, so it's a mystery to me what people do for a living in small towns."

"Not much," he admitted with a rueful smile. "Probably half the population commutes to Cleveland to work."

"Oh, is that what you do?"

"Yes, I'm a lab technician at a medical center."

"That sounds very interesting—"

Jane excused herself for interrupting, but Ross was still her guest and he had not yet had breakfast.

"What would you like to eat?" she asked.

"I can't ask you to cook for me. It's way past the time we agreed to have breakfast."

"Jane loves to cook any time of day or night," Ethel assured him.

"I was planning scrambled eggs and salmon, but I'm flexible. What's your favorite?"

"I love fried eggs swimming in butter. Margo doesn't think they're good for me, so I rarely have them."

"What if I cook them in a fat-free spray and season them just a bit to compensate for not using butter?"

"I guess she can't object to that," he said with a boyish grin.

"Is she coming down for breakfast?" Jane asked.

"She left some time ago. I guess she wanted to be in Potterston when the stores opened. She wants to get some things our daughter will need for college."

"Oh, you have a daughter leaving the nest," Ethel said. "I know what that's like. I had three children who grew up and left home. Do you have other children?"

"No, only the one."

"I cried for days when my youngest left," Ethel reminisced. "I just couldn't believe they were all gone."

Jane tried to turn her aunt away from this sensitive subject by offering her a plate of gingersnaps, but Ethel was almost unstoppable when she got going on a topic.

"Yes, my wife feels that way too," Ross said sadly.

"Well, don't you?" Ethel asked.

"Of course, I'll miss her like crazy. She's the sunshine in our house."

"I thought my life was over when the last child left. I felt that I wasn't useful anymore," Ethel said, surprising Jane with her admission, something she'd never brought up before.

"You have lots to do now," Jane said. "Friends, activities. And we love having you live near us."

"But that's now. Then I felt so deserted out on the farm, just the two of us."

"How did you get over it?" Ross asked.

"My husband was still alive then. I wasn't really alone. After all, it had just been the two of us before we had children. When I got used to the idea, it was sort of like a second honeymoon. Of course, at first he just pooh-poohed my missing the kids. That made me so mad. Then I realized that he missed them as much as I did. He didn't want to admit it—he didn't think it was manly or something. It made all the difference in the world to me when he confessed that it was hard on him too. My Bob was a good man."

"Yes, he was," Jane agreed. "It's so important to have at least one person to share your sorrow—and your happiness. I thank the Lord continually for you and Louise and Alice."

Ethel went on to other subjects, keeping up a lively

conversation even though Ross began answering her in monosyllables. He quickly finished his fried eggs and whole wheat toast, and then excused himself.

"He's a nice man," Ethel said when he had gone.

"Yes," Jane agreed, although she wondered why he had seemed suddenly so eager to leave. Aunt Ethel could be very chatty, but she was good-hearted. Most people found her at least mildly amusing. What she'd said about her own children leaving seemed to have bothered Ross.

"How long are he and his wife going to stay?" Ethel asked. Once her aunt met people, she liked to keep track of them.

"They're booked through this week," Jane said.

When Louise arrived in the jury room, most of her cojurors were enjoying coffee and freshly made cinnamon rolls that Eve Franken had brought.

"My mother-in-law made them," Eve said. "She absolutely adores baking. In fact, if she sits for my kids much longer, they're going to get roly-poly. She made three kinds of cookies yesterday. I'll bring some tomorrow. We'll never eat everything she's made at our house. Can you believe I've gained four pounds since I've been on jury duty?"

Louise couldn't see where she'd put on weight, but then, Eve was wearing a loose-fitting candy-striped pink and white shirt that concealed her figure. What Louise didn't like hearing was the offer to bring cookies tomorrow. Eve made it sound as though she was sure they would have to come back another day. How long did she expect their deliberations to last?

"I make a delicious sour cream coffee cake," Bertha Hayward said. "The folks I work with at the road commission love it when I make one for them. I thought of bringing one here, but I didn't know whether I should."

"Can we get started?" Egbert asked, frustration evident in the tone of his voice. "My business picked up three new customers last week. My brother-in-law has to go to a job service for temporary help every morning. I need to get back to work."

"Is everyone here?" Louise took a silent count. "Let's sit down, and we'll get started."

"I should hope so," Yvonne said.

"I want to tell you before we take a vote," Everett Eskridge said. "I've given it a lot of thought, and I've decided that Reddenhurst is guilty of embezzling from the department store. I'm still not so sure about the foundation."

"If he's a crook, he's a crook. I don't see the difference," Yvonne said. "You can't be so wishy-washy if we're ever going to get out of here."

This was exactly the kind of personal comment that Louise tried to discourage in her role as chairperson. It was counterproductive for jurors to criticize each other, not to mention unkind. In other similar situations, a gentle word from Louise or even a glance served to quiet the offender, but Yvonne was the hardest one to rein in. Before Louise could attempt to do so, Florence stepped up to defend Everett.

"Everyone has a right to his own opinion," she said emphatically.

Yvonne rolled her eyes but said nothing to Florence. There was something about the portly woman that intimidated even Yvonne.

The first vote of the day showed some progress, but not enough. Egbert had been persuaded to change his initial vote to guilty. With his change of heart, there were only three jurors voting not guilty: Bertha Hayward, Sterling Hagar and Ella Girard.

Louise didn't think Bertha would stand firm for acquittal if everyone else voted guilty. She had already acknowledged the validity of some of the prosecution's points. Sterling was harder to read. Since he was an accountant, he was in a unique position to interpret the more complicated aspects of the case. He was also obsessive in wanting to weigh every minute detail. He was the one who insisted on going over the testimony again and again, looking for possible loopholes and attorney errors. The rest of the jury was getting impatient with him.

Ella Girard looked especially careworn this morning, and her watery blue eyes seemed vacant while they went over now-familiar testimony. She would not speak up to explain or defend her position, so it was impossible to know her reasons for standing firm for acquittal. The one thing that seemed to interest her was how long Reddenhurst would be in jail if he was found guilty.

"That's up to the judge," Louise told her when she brought it up again.

"I imagine it will be a long, long time," Ella said in a distressed tone. "He's not a young man, you know."

Louise sighed and continued with the day's deliberations. The chemistry teacher didn't have anything to say this morning, but then, he'd made up his mind. He spent his time looking out the window or getting refills for his coffee and wandering around the room. Louise wondered whether he permitted his students to be so inattentive.

After allowing a reasonable time for discussion, she called for another vote, but she didn't have much hope for a unanimous decision.

Asking for Joanna's help with the library program hadn't turned out at all the way Alice had expected. Never mind that the young woman was a disaster at crafts. When she told a story, she tended to make comments that were above the comprehension of the children. Alice imagined that she would be outstanding with an older audience, but she didn't seem to have had any experience with youngsters.

"I have to give her a time limit today," Nia said when Alice arrived after work to lend support. "Children of this age have an attention span that's pretty short. If they're attentive for ten minutes, they're doing well. It took Joanna nearly half an hour to go through the book yesterday because she tried to explain the author's intention and other insights into the story. The kids were fidgeting and getting into mischief by the time she finished."

"She loves telling stories," Alice said, wondering how to limit Joanna's time without hurting her feelings. "I'll speak to her when she gets here. I'm sure time just gets away from her because she's so enthusiastic. Maybe I can give her a two-minute warning—hold up two fingers so she knows it's nearly time to stop. I'll check on her choice of story too."

"I would appreciate your doing that," Nia said. "Since the mothers came on such short notice, I hate to cut into their plans for crafts."

Alice tried to think of a creative, subtle way to tell Joanna that she had to shorten her storytelling. But by the time the woman arrived at the library, out of breath and close to the time the children would be dropped off, it seemed the only way was to be direct.

"It's important that you limit your story to ten minutes," Alice said. "Otherwise the mothers won't have time to do the things they've planned."

"Oh, no problem," Joanna said cheerfully. "I know that I get a bit carried away. Today I'm reading a cute little story about paper dolls. It's really short compared to yesterday's."

Alice wasn't at all sure the boys would appreciate a story about any kind of doll, especially after their reaction to the pantins, but Joanna did have a lively reading style. Maybe she could hold their attention for ten minutes.

"I'll give you a signal when your time is nearly up," Alice said. "When I hold up two fingers, that means you have two minutes left."

"That would be really helpful," Joanna said enthusiastically.

When the children started arriving, Nia had them sit in a circle on the floor facing a child-sized chair where Joanna was sitting to read her story. Her long skirt, a bright green cotton with yellow moons and stars dancing across the bottom, fanned out around her and made her appear to be in costume. She began reading as soon as all the children were there, which, fortunately, was very close to the appointed time.

"Hi, boys and girls. We have a new member of our group today," she said. "Remember when we made pantins on Monday? Well, I made a pantin, and he wants to join us for the story. Let's all say hello to Dancing Jack."

Most of the children dutifully complied, although the two older boys focused their attention on a pack of baseball cards that one pulled from his pocket. Nia relieved him of it before he could cause a disruption.

Joanna pulled on her string, and a paper puppet popped out of the book she was holding. Several children giggled, and Alice had to admit that the pantin was delightful. Joanna had given him a funny face, bright red spots on his cheeks and a mop of bright orange yarn hair. She'd also gone to some lengths to make real fabric clothes embellished with lots of little buttons and sequins. In fact, the clothing must have taken hours to make, not counting time to shop for all the odd bits she used.

As Joanna danced her creation in front of the children, Alice could see that she had definitely captured their attention this time. Now if she could only hold it for ten minutes.

"If you remember our discussion on Monday, you'll recall that in olden days paper dolls were not just for kids," she said, "but actually were adult toys first. They were so popular in places like

Paris that dressmakers who made clothes for ladies also designed clothes for dolls."

Joanna stood and walked around the circle, entertaining the children by dancing the pantin in front of some and on the heads of others. It was a nice display of puppetry, but Alice hoped she would get on with the story.

"By the time paper dolls were popular in the United States, they were just for kids. The first company to make a lot of paper dolls was McLoughlin Brothers in 1828. You could buy a whole set for five cents or ten cents. They had fun names like Dottie Dimple, Lottie Love and Jenny June. In the 1880s a man named Peter Thompson made sets with names like Pansy Blossom, Jessie Jingle, Lillie Lane and Bessie Bright. He even made Nellie Bly paper dolls, and she was a real person, a reporter. That was a very unusual occupation for a woman in those days."

Alice tried to signal Joanna to begin the story so she wouldn't run over her time, but she was in her own world.

"All those early paper dolls were printed in black and white. They had to be colored by hand. But in the 1870s and '80s, printers learned how to make things in color with lithographs. They used stones, one for each color. It was really complicated, but they made beautiful paper dolls of famous people like kings and queens and actresses. How many of you have paper dolls of famous people?"

When no children responded, Alice quietly whispered to Joanna that she begin the story, but she seemed not to hear Alice.

"When I was little," Joanna continued, "I loved cutting the

ladies out of catalogs and making my own clothes for them. Of course, some magazines printed paper dolls, and so did comic books and newspapers."

One of the bigger boys nudged another, and Nia had to step in to stop their giggling disturbance.

"Please read the story now," Alice said more loudly this time, after walking behind Joanna and whispering directly in her ear.

The story, it turned out, was one of Joanna's originals.

"Princess Peony was the most beautiful little girl in the world and the richest, but she was very, very unhappy."

Joanna's face crumpled in sorrow, then she went on to explain that the girl couldn't do any of the things that normal children did such as run, jump, dance or sing. She had to be perfect, sitting like a lady on her golden throne.

Alice had to admit that the story was enchanting, and Joanna acted out the parts with empathy and enthusiasm. In the end, Princess Peony's parents realized that she needed to have some childish fun. They hired a kindly peasant woman with several active children to come to the castle with her family and play games. Even the king and queen joined in, and laughter was heard coming from the castle for the first time.

Unfortunately, as good as the story was, Joanna took twice her allotted time to reach the conclusion, totally ignoring Alice's two-minute warning. By then, even the formerly most rapt members of her audience had started to squirm, and Nia had to remove the two boisterous boys from the circle of children for their disruptive behavior.

Alice felt sick at heart. She knew Joanna meant well, but she couldn't let her ruin a program that the ANGELs had worked so hard to plan. Somehow, she had to make sure that the children still wanted to come next week. There were two days left in this week. Someone else would have to read the story.

Nia agreed when they had a whispered conference. Joanna's stories were fine, but they didn't inspire the listeners to check out books to take home. Joanna gave lip service to changing, then went ahead and did exactly as she wanted.

When Alice suggested that the librarian read for the rest of the week, Nia was pleased to do it—and somewhat relieved. Unfortunately, Alice would have to tell Joanna.

The two of them rode home together, and Alice struggled to find a way to break the bad news.

"I really appreciate all the effort you've put into the library program," Alice said. "Your stories are charming. It's difficult to hold the attention of children so young."

"I love doing it."

That wasn't what Alice wanted to hear. She tried again.

"The problem is, there's only a very short time for a story. The children expect refreshments and a craft, and they need some outdoor time whenever possible."

"My story was too long today, wasn't it? I'm really sorry. I'll do better tomorrow."

"Joanna, Nia and I decided that it might be better if she reads the story tomorrow. She has some new books that she would like to introduce to the children. It's not that you're not a wonderful reader."

"Oh."

Alice heard the disappointment in that single syllable.

"I should have read the story she wanted. It just sounded so lame. There must be a million books about a boy and his dog. I don't even like dogs. I was bitten by our neighbor's dog when I was little. I still have a scar on my ankle."

"You're a very good reader, but the idea behind the program is to promote use of the library."

"Oh well."

"I'm really sorry."

"Don't worry. It was fun while it lasted. This isn't the first time I've been fired. Or can a volunteer be fired? Dismissed, relieved of duty, replaced, downsized—"

"You were sweet to help out," Alice assured her.

"Deactivated, decommissioned—no, that makes me sound like a battleship. You know, it would be fun to write a poem about all the ways to be eased out of a job: replaced, retired, kicked out..."

Alice shook her head sadly. She felt terrible, but sometimes a person had to do what was asked. As a nurse, she knew the dire consequences of not following procedures.

"Discharged, let go, made obsolete. No, I don't think the synonyms have quite the right ring for a poem. Maybe I won't bother."

Alice tried to think of something that would soothe Joanna's feelings, but sometimes words just weren't sufficient.

Chapter Thirteen

"Has everyone gone to bed?" Alice asked, coming into the kitchen as Jane was doing a few last-minute chores.

"As far as I know. Louise is exhausted. She feels like a prisoner, cooped up all day with a group of people who can't come to a unanimous decision."

"Does she think it will be a hung jury?" Alice asked.

"She's worried that it might be. I'm afraid she'll take it as a personal failure if they have to go back to the judge without a decision, although I don't know what she can do to change other people's minds. It's still nine to three in favor of conviction."

"Imagine being confined to a room in the courthouse on such a lovely day. I think I'll have breakfast and then go for a long walk. Have you seen Joanna? I'm a bit worried about her."

"I was wondering why she missed dinner, but I haven't seen her this evening. What's up with her?"

"I'm afraid I know," Alice said sadly.

"What's wrong?" Jane stopped what she was doing and gave her sister a puzzled look.

"I had to remove her from the library program. I feel terrible about it, but she just wouldn't do what Nia wanted. She lost the children's attention by making her stories way too long."

"You fired her as a library volunteer?" Jane sounded incredulous.

"I didn't want to, but the children were getting restless and unruly. If they don't have fun this week, it's unlikely many will be back next week. The ANGELs would be devastated if they couldn't present the program that they've worked so hard to put together. And Nia would be very disappointed too. She's counting on the program to bring more children into the library."

"So Joanna refused to get with the program?"

"I don't think it was a refusal, but she certainly didn't take advice. She's inexperienced in working with young children, and she didn't realize how short their attention span is."

"I hate to think that she's staging a hunger strike," Jane said with a worried expression. "I'll make up a tray, so she can have a late-night snack."

"I should take it to her. I'm the one who hurt her feelings."

"All right. Let me think what she might like. She doesn't exactly have a hearty appetite, but I think one of my oatmeal cookies might hit the spot. I can throw together some fruit for a salad, and we have an individual serving of yogurt in the fridge. And a little pot of hot tea might be nice too."

"That sounds fine," Alice said. "I should say something to her, but I'm not sure what."

"I don't think you had a choice about the library. Cynthia is the one who has my sympathy. It can't be easy working with Joanna on a day-to-day basis."

Alice sighed and waited while Jane prepared a pretty wooden

tray with painted daisies by adding a bright yellow napkin and a daffodil in a bud vase. She hoped Jane's cheerful offering would please their guest.

Alice carried the tray upstairs, not knowing what to expect. Was Joanna angry or hurt? Or did her absence at dinner mean that she was busy on one of her poems? Alice said a silent prayer, hoping that Joanna wasn't taking the library incident as a personal rejection.

With the tray in hand, she couldn't knock on the door. Instead she called Joanna's name several times. There was no response.

She could have gone out, or she might still be sleeping. Maybe she was listening to music with earphones.

Or she could be angry. Or sick.

Alice put the tray on the floor and knocked, first softly, then hard enough to make her knuckles sting.

"Joanna!"

"I just ran out for a minute," Joanna said softly, coming up behind Alice and startling her. "I wanted to check the mailbox in case no one checked it today. But even in the dark, I could feel that it's empty."

"Oh dear," Alice said, regaining her composure. "I'm sure Jane always checks it when it comes in the early afternoon."

"I'll check again tomorrow then."

Alice was blocking the way to her room, but Joanna made no move to get around her.

"I brought you a snack. If it's not enough, Jane's kitchen is always open. You were missed at dinner tonight."

"Thank you," she said. "It's very nice of you."

"Can we talk a moment?" Alice asked, dreading what needed to be said.

"Sure. Do you want to come in?"

Alice nodded and retrieved the tray, carrying it inside and setting it down.

"About yesterday," she began.

"No problem. My mom wanted me to get a teaching degree, but I always knew I didn't want to work with little kids as she does. I think you have to be born to teach the early grades. She was. The kids in her classes adore her. You should have seen our house at Christmas, plates of cookies, little gifts like potholders and ornaments. I bet my mother has enough decorations from her students to cover the White House tree."

"You're a good reader," Alice said, afraid the words sounded a little lame. "It's just that young children can only listen so long before they get restless."

"I guess I know that now. I thought it was a good opportunity to try out some of the stories I've written, but I'd better stick to poetry. You know what Polonius said to his son, Laertes: 'This above all: to thine own self be true, and it must follow, as the night the day, thou canst not then be false to any man.'"

"Yes, I remember that good advice," Alice said.

"Of course, I prefer Shakespeare's sonnets. So many of his plays end badly. Have you read *Titus Andronicus*? What horrible people they were! A bunch of his sons died fighting the Goths, so he murdered Queen Tamora's oldest son to get even. From there the whole play is ghastly. Her two bad sons did terrible things to his daughter, and the entire revenge thing ends with them being served to her in a pie. Yuck!"

"It does sound like an unpleasant play," Alice agreed, wondering whether this was Joanna's way of saying she didn't hold a grudge.

"'To give away yourself keeps yourself still, and you must live, drawn by your own sweet skill.' That's Shakespeare's Sonnet Sixteen."

When Joanna recited poetry, her face took on an angelic cast. The words of great poets seemed to carry her to another dimension, something Alice observed even if she didn't completely understand it.

"I'm glad you're not upset about the library," Alice said, hoping it had been Joanna's intent to tell her that.

"No, that wasn't why I missed dinner. When I'm in a creative mood, I sometimes forget to eat." She looked at the offerings on the tray. "Jane is such a good cook. It's a shame to waste her food on me. Give me bread, apples, cheese and an occasional can of tuna, and I'm content."

"I'm sure Jane doesn't see it as wasted time. Try the oatmeal cookie anyway," Alice said. "You must be famished after missing dinner."

Alice left the room, leaving Joanna to her snack, but she wondered whether Joanna really had gotten over her disappointment about the library program.

"Oh, Alice," Joanna called after her, "please be sure to remind Jane that I'm expecting a letter."

"Whoever gets the mail will be certain to give it to you," Alice assured her, trying not to be curious about her urgency.

Jane and Cynthia had lunch together. Jane enjoyed having her niece all to herself. Since they were only sixteen years apart in age, Jane sometimes felt more like a big sister than an aunt.

Cynthia was a light eater, and loved a good salad for lunch. Jane knew spinach salad was one of her favorites. She tossed baby spinach with thinly sliced raw mushrooms and grated hard-boiled eggs, then crumbled some strips of crisply fried bacon. She wanted a dressing that complemented the natural flavors but didn't overwhelm them. The answer was a recipe she often used for family meals—vegetable oil with just a touch of sesame oil, sugar and Dijon mustard. She added lemon juice, freshly ground pepper and a pinch of salt. To complete the meal, she made bite-sized corn muffins. She loved the recipe, which called for creamed corn and sour cream, producing a moist, flavorful muffin.

They'd agreed to have lunch at twelve thirty, and like her mother, Cynthia was prompt, arriving in the kitchen at exactly that time.

Cynthia gave the blessing, a familiar one that she had learned as a child: "God is great, God is good, let us thank Him for our food."

They smiled at each other, recalling the special times when they'd shared family meals years ago.

"How is your work going?" Jane asked as they talked a mile a minute, almost forgetting to eat.

"Mine is fine, but I'm very worried about Joanna's. She knows the guidelines for the books we publish, but she always wants to embellish them with her own ideas. I've had a very upset author on the phone this morning. If she were to do all the revisions Joanna asked for, the book would be double the length and have little resemblance to the original."

"What can you do about it?"

"Technically, I'm still her boss. I had a long talk with her after the call, but she just doesn't get it. The art department is in limbo waiting for the final text, marketing is howling and the chance of getting her book to the printer on time is diminishing. I shouldn't talk about a fellow employee, but I'm at my wit's end. You have a sympathetic ear, and I know you'll keep anything I tell you confidential. I have to talk to someone, and Mother has too much on her plate right now."

"Yes, jury duty has been more demanding than she expected."

"Do you know where Joanna is? She seems to have disappeared."

"No, I don't. In fact, I went upstairs to invite her to join us for lunch, but she wasn't in her room. I checked the rest of the house and the front porch."

"Whatever she's doing, it probably has nothing to do with saving her job."

"I'm just sorry your visit has been so stressful," Jane said. "Is there anything I can do?"

"Afraid not. This salad is wonderful, by the way. I'd love to have your recipe for the dressing."

"I'll run off a copy. I'm gradually putting my favorite recipes on the computer, especially those I've made up or drastically altered. You can go through my file and see if there are any others you would like—if you have time."

"That would be great if I can get to it. Maybe tonight. I would like to spend more time with Mother. I'm concerned about her. She didn't expect jury duty to last anywhere near this long, and I can tell it's wearing on her."

"How could it not!"

"Maybe they'll have a breakthrough today."

"I pray they will," Jane said fervently.

Alice went to the library again to lend moral support to Nia, although she felt a bit rushed after hurrying there from work in Potterston. On the way, she stopped by Nine Lives to check on a book she'd ordered, expecting it to take two minutes at most. As it happened, Viola was in a chatty mood.

"Alice, I'm glad you stopped by," she said.

"Don't tell me Wendell has been into mischief."

"No, nothing like that. He's being a perfect guest. I just wondered whether Joanna is still with you."

"Yes, I expect she'll be with us until Cynthia leaves."

"She's such a lovely young woman. It's so rare to find someone who really appreciates the nineteenth-century poets. Since talking to her, I've been rereading many of my favorites."

"She'll be happy to hear that."

"I've been hoping she would stop in again. I bought a box of old books and magazines at an auction, mainly because I spotted a periodical that had the first appearance of one of Bret Harte's stories. When I got the box home, the periodical I wanted wasn't in it. Apparently someone had stolen it or moved it to another box. People do that at auctions sometimes. I should have stood right by the box until it came up for bid. At least the lot turned out to be a reasonably good buy even without the Bret Harte story."

"It must be exciting for you to go to auctions looking for books," Alice said.

"Yes, I love it, although there's a lot of competition for real rarities. One of the books in the box was a volume of poetry by Dante Gabriel Rossetti, the painter. You've heard of him, haven't you?"

"The name, yes, but I couldn't tell you anything about him."

"He was one of the founders of the Pre-Raphaelite Brotherhood, a group that wanted to go back to the bold, vivid style of painting before Raphael. His paintings are in many important museums."

"Raphael is an artist I've heard of," Alice said with a smile. "He painted breathtakingly beautiful religious pictures."

"Well, Rossetti was a poet as well as a painter. The book I found isn't a first edition, but it's in nice condition, and I'd like to give it to Joanna as a reminder of her visit in Acorn Hill."

"I'm sure it would mean a lot to her."

"You might mention that I would like to see her before she leaves."

"I'll certainly do that," Alice said, pleased that Joanna had made a good impression on Viola.

As she hurried to the library, she mused over Joanna's foibles and strengths. Alice thought of her standing at a fork in the road, not sure which way to go. She could probably be perfectly happy immersing herself in the world of poetry, but the chance of a poet making a living from what he or she wrote was slim.

Alice realized how fortunate she was to have a career she loved. She'd never been indecisive about what she wanted to do. How difficult it must be for Joanna, who seemingly had no one to support and encourage her poetic efforts. It was amazing that she could maintain her enthusiasm.

She glanced at her watch on her way into the library, not surprised to see that she was a few minutes late. From the doorway, the library seemed too quiet. She didn't hear children's voices. She walked toward the children's section, a pleasant area by the front windows where open shelves painted in bright primary colors formed a three-sided reading area. The tables were arranged in a row again, and every seat was occupied by a child silently engrossed in listening.

Alice blinked in surprise. Joanna was reading to them, and even the unruly older boys were giving her their full attention.

Nia was standing off to the left along with two mothers who had come to help. Alice walked over to them, full of questions but not wanting to interrupt the reading.

The librarian must have read her face. She motioned for Alice to follow her into the adult reading area where they wouldn't be heard.

"I didn't have the heart to say no when she asked for one more chance," Nia said with a helpless shrug. "She was willing to use a book of my choice and not take a second over ten minutes. As you can see, she really does have a gift for reading to children when she's focused."

"Yes, I see. Joanna is certainly full of surprises."

She waited until the program ended, pleased that Joanna helped with the crafts without inserting any of her own creative touches into the making of clay figurines. Not only that, she took responsibility for washing the tables after the children went outside to play a game. Alice was proud of her but still puzzled. What had brought about this drastic change?

"Wait for me," Joanna said to Alice as the children filed back inside to wait for parents to claim them. "We can go back to the inn together."

"You did a lovely job today," Alice said as they rode home after stopping at Nine Lives so that Viola could give Joanna her good-bye gift. Alice was glad she hadn't had time to leave the car at the inn when the day's light rain turned into a deluge.

"I felt terrible about letting you down," Joanna said after a few minutes of silence as Alice parked the car at home. "You've been so nice to me. I'm happy that the librarian gave me another chance."

"Yes, so am I," Alice agreed, but her mind was wandering to Joanna's job. Would the woman be able to mend her ways in time to save the position? Joanna had an immense store of talent, but it seemed to take a lot to motivate her. At least she didn't bear a grudge for being fired from the library program. It had been a wakeup call, but what would it take for her to focus all her efforts on doing work for the publisher who employed her?

Alice couldn't decipher the enigma that was Joanna.

Louise's head was pounding. At least Florence was driving so she could close her eyes and try to let the day's tension drift away.

"I'm getting a little tired of traipsing over to the courthouse every day," Florence said. "I have so many other things to do. Do you think the jury will ever agree on a decision?"

"We made progress today," Louise said, wearily opening her eyes.

"Yes, Sterling decided that the man is guilty. Why it took him so long, I'll never know."

Louise listened to Florence's replay of the arguments that had filled their day.

"He's a very cautious man," she said, although she shared Florence's impatience with his wavering.

"Well, I don't think being an accountant should mean weighing every word of the long, boring testimony a hundred times. If anything, he should have realized right away that Reddenhurst was cooking the books. I didn't trust him from the first minute I saw him."

"I know it's tempting, but we jurors can't make decisions based on how the defendant looks," Louise offered mildly, knowing that Florence was too wrapped up in what she was saying to pay much attention.

"What surprised me was that Bertha Haywood changed her mind as soon as Sterling did. She made it pretty plain that she thought jury duty was a vacation from her road commission job. Maybe even she is tired of being cooped up in that room all day."

"Perhaps." Louise felt that she needed to say something so Florence knew she was listening.

"I think Yvonne would vote to hang the man if she could. I wonder why she's so angry all the time. I feel a bit sorry for Reddenhurst. He made bad choices, but he knows how much he's lost. People may find it hard to respect him again, even if he doesn't go to jail."

"Yes, that's true." Like Florence, Louise was at a loss about the Realtor's negative attitude. And, she thought Florence was being unusually insightful about the defendant.

"I never thought being a juror could be so complicated," Florence said. "Why do you suppose Ella Girard is holding out against all the rest of us? I thought she was such a little mouse when I first met her. All she does is fret over inconsequential things. I swear, she worries more about the weather than any human being I've ever met, and she lives within walking distance of the courthouse. She doesn't have to drive back and forth every day."

They were driving in a drizzle, the dark sky threatening heavier rain.

"Let's list what we know about her," Florence said in a take-charge voice. "Not much, I'm afraid."

"She's never given a good reason for voting not guilty. In fact, you would think that Reddenhurst was a relative or something. She doesn't like to hear anything bad about him."

"Maybe she just has a kind nature."

"She isn't being kind to the rest of us by being so stubborn. I had a nightmare about telling the judge that we can't reach a decision."

"It's hard to deal with a worrier," Louise said thoughtfully.

"If I were the foreperson, I would take her aside and find out what her problem is," Florence said, still sounding a little miffed that she hadn't been selected for the position.

"Yes, I should do that."

Louise was surprised to hear herself agreeing with Florence. The trouble was that she didn't know how to go about approaching Ella. The woman never gave a reason for her stance, and she was unmoved by argument. In fact, most of the time she seemed to be somewhere else, her eyes vacant and her expression bemused. She didn't drop off to sleep, but her mind seemed miles away from the deliberations.

"Today's lunch wasn't as good as it usually is," Florence said. "I didn't like the egg salad at all. I always add a dab of mustard and some spices to give mine a little zest. Do you suppose they're trying to starve us into agreeing on a decision?"

Louise laughed even though it made her head feel worse. "The caterers don't care how long we take. It's good business for them to keep bringing our lunches."

"I suppose you're right," Florence said in a grudging voice. "But if we can't reach a unanimous decision tomorrow, I think we should vote on whether to tell the judge that we can't agree. People can't put their lives on hold indefinitely."

Louise had been thinking along that line herself, but she

didn't want self-interest to enter into her decision. Cynthia wouldn't be at the inn much longer, and Louise would very much like to get home early tomorrow to be with her. However, before she could suggest a deadlock to the other jurors, she had to be absolutely sure that the situation was hopeless.

"Well, I'll see you tomorrow," Florence said when she dropped off Louise in front of the inn.

"Tomorrow and tomorrow and tomorrow," Louise said glumly. "Perhaps someday we'll look back on this as a good learning experience."

"Humph."

Florence drove away as soon as the car door was shut.

"Louise!"

She saw that Alice and Joanna had come out to meet her on the front porch. "You're awfully late today. Did the jury reach a decision?" her sister asked.

"No, unfortunately, but we're down to one holdout."

She started to ask Joanna how her day had been, but the young woman had streaked over to the mailbox, moving faster than Alice had ever seen her move before and ignoring the downpour.

"Jane would have gotten the mail before now," Alice called out to her.

"Oh yes, I suppose she would have," Joanna said, running up the front porch steps and into the house.

"What do you suppose she's expecting?" Alice asked.

Louise shook her head. This was just one more puzzling thing about their resident poet.

Louise found Joanna alone in the kitchen Friday morning. She was rather listlessly picking at the contents of a custard cup, her attention riveted on a slender, worn-looking book in front of her on the table.

She looked startled when Louise said, "Good morning."

"Oh, I didn't hear you coming. Viola gave me this little volume of Rossetti poems. My mother always says that I can't hear a tornado coming when I have my nose in a book." She tossed aside a stray lock of hair.

"Don't let me interrupt. I'm just going to have a quick breakfast and be on my way."

"Oh, Jane said to be sure to tell you there's a serving of eggs Lorraine for you. Just pop it in the oven to reheat it. She didn't want you dashing off for jury duty without a good breakfast."

"Where is she?" Louise asked.

"I think she said something about getting her car serviced."

Louise opened the already heated oven and put in the luscious serving of eggs. Jane had made one of Louise's favorites—eggs with minced bacon, Gruyère cheese and a bit of cream baked in a custard cup set in a water bath. She poured herself some juice and joined Joanna at the table, silently saying grace.

"I like to start the day by reading," Joanna said after a few minutes, rousing herself from deep concentration on the book. "You would be surprised how often I find a thought that stays with me all day."

Louise smiled at her earnest words, understanding exactly what she meant. She liked to read her Bible before beginning the day, finding strength and inspiration in the beloved passages. Unfortunately her mind was in such turmoil this morning thinking about the possibility of a hung jury that she scarcely remembered what she had read.

She retrieved her eggs from the oven and ate as much as she could. She put the remainder in the trash container, discreetly concealing the food under her paper napkin. She didn't want to hurt her sister's feelings, but she had lost her appetite as she thought about another day at the courthouse.

"What are your plans for today?" she asked Joanna just to fill the silence in the room.

"Mine?" Joanna looked surprised. "Oh, I expect there will be some jobs I have to do. I hope the mailman brings me a letter. Have you ever noticed how slow the mail is when you're expecting something?"

"It's a conspiracy," Louise said with a laugh, bringing a smile to the younger woman's face.

"What about you? Do you think this will be your last day in court?"

"I sincerely hope so."

"I never got to the deliberation part of jury duty. Whatever do you do all day, now that the trial part is over?"

"We discuss." Perhaps argue might be a more accurate description, Louise thought.

"Well, good luck. I've heard of trials that lasted weeks and even months. If I were the defendant, I would want to get it over with as quickly as possible. Imagine, waiting all that time to hear whether or not you had to go to jail."

"Yes, it would be very stressful," Louise agreed. "Now I'd better get going. It's not a long drive, but I like to allow plenty of time."

"My mother would love you. She always gets every place at least fifteen minutes early. Think of all the time she's wasted waiting for something to happen. It must add up to years now that she's old."

Louise smiled, imagining that she must also seem very old to Joanna. It never ceased to amaze her that she didn't regard herself any differently now than she had thirty years ago. *Younger people assume that senior citizens are somehow different, but in truth, the essence of a person doesn't change with age,* Louise thought.

"I'll see you this evening," Louise said as she left the kitchen.

"Have a nice day," Joanna called after her.

Louise was driving alone this morning. Florence wanted to take her own car and stay in Potterston to do some errands, so Louise had opted to go separately.

Although she didn't want to talk about the case anymore, Louise did miss having a companion on the drive. The responsibility for bringing the jury's deliberations to a close weighed heavily on her mind. She would have welcomed any distraction.

Several cars and a bread van passed her on the highway, and she was surprised to note how slowly she was driving. It wasn't like her to delay an unpleasant appointment, so she increased to her normal safe speed, trying to focus completely on the task of driving.

One of the real hardships of jury duty was that she couldn't talk about the case with the people who mattered most to her. She realized that a feeling of isolation was one of the burdens of being a juror.

"Dear Lord," she prayed aloud, "This isn't like me. I'm never really alone. You're always with me." She recited words from the most comforting of all Psalms:

> *"'The LORD is my shepherd, I shall not be in want. He makes me lie down in green pastures, he leads me beside quiet waters, he restores my soul. He guides me in paths of righteousness for his name's sake'" (Psalm 23:1–3).*

She felt calmer as she neared Potterston. She'd prayed that she and the other jury members would act in the name of fairness and not expediency, that whatever they decided, it would be just, upholding the law of the land, but also compassionate.

As she walked toward the courthouse from the parking lot, she spotted another juror walking on the sidewalk that ran beside the lot. Ella Girard was carrying an oversized black umbrella and a big gray shoulder bag, seemingly prepared for whatever the day would bring.

Louise hurried toward the woman, feeling that God had given her this chance to resolve the problem of a lone juror holding fast for acquittal. If nothing else, at least she would understand Ella's reasoning.

"Good morning, Ella."

"Oh, Mrs. Smith. Good morning." She was the only person on the jury who never called anyone by their first name.

"I wondered if we could talk for a moment."

Ella's pale skin seemed to turn even whiter. She looked on both sides of Louise as though hoping for rescue.

"We won't be late, I promise you. Come sit in my car for a minute."

Louise shepherded her to the Cadillac and opened the passenger door for her. When Ella was seated, Louise went to the other side and sat behind the wheel.

"First, I want you to know that I respect your right to make your own decision about the case. I don't want you to go against your principles or your conscience."

Ella didn't say anything. She wasn't going to make this easy. If Louise was correctly reading the expression on her face, she was feeling intimidated.

"It's very hard to make a decision that could send a man to prison," Louise continued. "Of course, it's up to the judge to decide Mr. Reddenhurst's punishment, if we convict him. We can only give our best possible judgment about his guilt or innocence."

Still, Ella didn't respond, so Louise plunged on.

"What makes this difficult is that none of the other jurors understands why you're so sure Mr. Reddenhurst is innocent. It would help immensely if we knew what you're thinking."

"I'm not one to talk much," Ella said defensively.

"That's your right also. I'm not here to bully you into

changing your mind. I only want to know the reason why you think he's not guilty."

Louise spoke softly and smiled gently, sensing the struggle Ella was having.

"You're very brave to stand for what you believe when no one else agrees with you," Louise went on when the other woman stayed silent. "It takes a strong person to do that."

"I just can't believe Mr. Reddenhurst would cheat people out of their money. I have such wonderful memories of going to his store when I was a child. My grandmother used to take me to the tearoom as a special treat. It was a wonderful place with beautiful crystal chandeliers and little, round tables. They had such lovely lunches, chicken salad and watercress sandwiches with no crust, and plates of whipped cream pastries. There were white linen tablecloths and a flower in a bud vase on every table. The waitresses wore blue and white striped uniforms with white caps and hairnets. It was like stepping into another world, so different from the one I lived in."

"You have wonderful memories of that time," Louise said in an encouraging voice.

"Oh yes. My father died quite young. He was a coal miner, and that work is so dangerous. My mother took me to Philadelphia to live with her sister's family. In those days there were no pensions for miners' widows. My aunt had four children of her own, all girls, and my cousins didn't really want my mother and me living there. My grandmother lived in the same city. She was quite elderly, but she understood how it was to live in a home where you're not wanted. My cousins resented it, but sometimes she took just me to Reddenhurst's Department Store for a special treat."

"I can see why you have wonderful memories of those excursions with your grandmother," Louise said gently.

"Yes, it wasn't easy for her to get around. She had arthritis and walked with a cane. She had to take a bus to come get me, then another to go to Reddenhurst's. Even when I was quite young, I could see how hard it was for her. She told me once that she wished I could live with her, but she only had a tiny one-bedroom apartment."

"I imagine that knowing how hard the trips were for her made your excursions even more special."

"Yes, she died when I was only twelve, and I've never stopped missing her."

"I understand, but do you think you would have enjoyed your lunches with your grandmother just as much if she'd taken you to another restaurant?"

"She loved the tearoom. She always took me there."

"Yes, but tell me this. Was it the tearoom or the time with your grandmother that was so special?"

Ella was silent for a long moment, and Louise was conscious of the need to get to the courthouse.

"I've never thought of it that way," she said at last.

"I'm sure Reddenhurst's tearoom was a lovely place, but Edward Reddenhurst sold it. He let his family's business go in exchange for money. Now the jury has to decide as a whole whether he did indeed steal from both the store and the foundation that was set up to help people."

"We have to go," Ella said urgently, looking at the ornate watch pinned on the bodice of her gray dress. "We mustn't be late."

"Please, at least think about whether Reddenhurst is guilty of embezzlement. If you have any questions, don't be afraid to ask them. I think you'll feel better about yourself if you're sure your decision is based on the facts of the case and not on a lovely memory."

Louise couldn't think of anything else to say. If she hadn't persuaded Ella to change her vote, there was nothing more she could do. At least now she had some understanding of the reason for the woman's stance.

Ella scurried out of the car and rushed toward the courthouse, leaving Louise behind. She watched her go with a heavy heart, not at all sure whether her words had meant a thing to the hold-out juror.

In the jury room things were much as they had been every day that week. Egbert was restlessly pacing, complaining. Lee had just helped himself to his second cream-filled frosted doughnut, and Ella was hovering near the window as though afraid to join the others in getting morning coffee. It was time to begin.

"Let's all sit down," Louise urged.

"Yes, let's sit and waste another day," Yvonne said.

Louise didn't want to react to the tirade that followed, but she knew the negative outburst was bad for the morale of the jurors.

"What I'd like to know, Ella," Yvonne addressed the older woman, who seemed to shrink in her chair as the Realtor spoke, "is why you're so blind? Anyone can see that Reddenhurst is guilty.

If it weren't for you, we could get this over with. You should be disqualified for mental incompetence."

Ella looked as though she'd been struck. Louise opened her mouth to defend her, but help came from an unexpected source.

"She's got a right to her opinion," Egbert said. "You're one to talk. You decided he was guilty before the trial even started."

The jurors exploded in an outburst of angry comments, so many people talking at once that it was hard to tell what the consensus was.

"Enough, please!" Louise surprised herself at the volume of her voice.

Perhaps because she was usually soft-spoken, her command got the attention of the others. When the room was silent, she outlined firmly what they had to do.

"I think we've passed beyond arguments. It's time to take a final vote. If it's not unanimous, then we have little choice but to go back to the judge and tell him that we can't agree."

She heard murmurs of agreement on all sides.

"We'll take a written vote," she said, again relieved that no one protested. In fact, the room was so quiet that a horn honking on the street below seemed intrusive. "Put your decision about the store first, then the foundation."

When the squares of white paper had been distributed, Florence was the first to pick up a pen and hastily scribble on it. She folded her paper in half with her short, pudgy fingers and kept her eyes riveted on the table.

Louise collected the ballots herself but asked Sterling Hagar to tally them. He methodically made a pile in front of himself on the table. She knew he would make a slow job of it, but the jury looked to him when it came to any kind of accounting. They sat in respectful silence while he opened the first one.

"On the first count, guilty. On the second count, guilty," he said in a serious voice.

There was no reaction from the others.

He read the second and the third ballots, both guilty on the two counts.

"I should think so," Yvonne muttered.

Everett Eskridge frowned at her. "I think you've had your say, Yvonne. Let him finish the count."

There was so much tension in the room that it seemed hard to breathe. Sterling had opened ten ballots, reading off the results. All were guilty votes.

Louise was in the grip of suspense, but Sterling couldn't be rushed. Nor would she try to hurry him along.

"Guilty on the first count, guilty on the second," he said, reaching for the twelfth and final ballot.

All eyes went to Ella Girard, assuming that this ballot was hers. She kept her eyes riveted on the tabletop in front of her.

Louise was afraid some of the jurors would explode in anger if Ella had indeed stuck with her faith in Reddenhurst's innocence. She was especially concerned about Yvonne, but Barry Hudson also wore an angry expression. Once his mind had been made up, he became adamant about Reddenhurst's guilt. He wouldn't like a hung jury at all.

Sterling looked up from the paper he was holding. "Guilty on the first count, guilty on the second count."

Everyone sat in stunned silence for a moment, then there were congratulations on all sides. They had a verdict.

Several jurors congratulated Ella for her vote change, but she withdrew into her shell, seemingly overwhelmed by the turmoil around her.

When they were back in the courtroom, Louise expected to be nervous acting as spokesperson for the jury. Quite on the contrary, she was so relieved to be able to give a unanimous decision that she was calm and confident.

Edward Reddenhurst didn't look at the jury after she read their decision. He didn't speak to his attorneys or look behind him for the woman who wasn't there. His face seemed gray, and his posture suggested defeat. Louise had a moment of pity for him and silently prayed for his redemption, but she remained convinced that the jury's decision was just.

After they were dismissed, the jury members lingered outside the courtroom door, seemingly needing something more. Eve and Mona hugged, promising to see each other again soon. Yvonne lingered on the fringes instead of rushing away as Louise would have expected her to do. Even Egbert stayed for a little garden talk with Lee.

Louise felt that something should be said, although the judge had already thanked them for their service.

"It's been a privilege to serve with all of you," she said, capturing their attention. "I think you all can be proud."

"I guess it's all right for us to go then?" Florence said.

"Yes, of course," Louise answered even though she knew they didn't need to be dismissed by her.

"I'm so glad I met all of you," Bertha Haywood said, surprising Sterling by giving him a big hug.

Then there were hugs all around; even Ella was included in the show of affection. Her face was flushed when Louise came to her, and she whispered a soft thank-you.

Egbert left first, followed by Yvonne, and then the others gradually moved toward the stairs to leave the courthouse.

"It was quite an experience," Florence said to Louise before she left. "I can't wait to tell the ladies at the chapel all about it."

Louise smiled. No doubt Florence's jury duty would give her something to talk about throughout the summer.

"I wish I knew whether he's going to prison," Eve said. "Leaving now is sort of like skipping the last chapter of a book."

"There will be a sentencing hearing in a week or so," Louise reminded her. "No doubt the results will be in the newspaper."

On the drive home alone, Louise found herself thinking about Edward Reddenhurst. He'd started life with opportunities that few others enjoyed, but somewhere along the line he'd made very bad choices. She didn't believe that he should escape punishment, but his ruined life made her very sad.

Jane was in the kitchen fixing a salad for lunch when she got home.

"Wonderful! You're home early. Does that mean the trial is over?"

"Yes, it's over. The jury brought in a guilty verdict."

"It must have been hard for you to decide he was guilty," Jane said sympathetically. "I know what a kind heart you have." Jane hugged her sister.

The trial was over, but Louise knew that it would be on her mind for some time to come. Perhaps the most awful part of the trial was witnessing Reddenhurst's abandonment by the unnamed woman inside the courtroom. After she failed to appear to support him, his arrogance faded, and he didn't seem to care about the verdict.

Louise thanked the Lord for her own loving family and their understanding.

Chapter Fourteen

"You haven't seen Joanna, have you?" Alice asked, enjoying a leisurely start on her regular day off.

She came into the kitchen as Jane was finishing her lunch.

"No, apparently she had breakfast while we were taking the car to be serviced, but I haven't seen her at all today."

"I brought in the mail. There's a letter for her."

"She'll be happy about that. She's been looking for it. Would you like some lunch?"

"Oh no, thank you. I dropped off some health pamphlets that I ordered for Vera to use in her class. She invited me to eat with her in the school lunchroom. That was an experience, eating goulash with a little plastic fork and drinking milk from a carton through a straw, but the children were fun. I should have told you not to make lunch for me, but it was a spur-of-the-minute thing."

"No problem. The good news is that Louise finished jury duty. She got home around noon."

"I'm so happy for her. She was really distressed that the jury couldn't come to a decision. Did they find the man guilty?"

"Yes, although I know that part of it didn't make her happy."

"No, I'm sure it didn't, but if Louise was convinced by the evidence, it was undoubtedly the right verdict. Where is she?"

"She and Cynthia went out to do some errands. They thought they'd probably stop somewhere for lunch."

"That's good," Alice said. "It's nearly time for Cynthia to leave, and they haven't had all that much time together. What can I do to help you today?"

"Why don't you take the afternoon off and do something fun? I'm pretty much caught up on everything that needs to be done, thanks to you."

"You know I enjoy working around the inn. Speaking of which, are your bird-watchers going to stay much longer? I really haven't had much chance to visit with them."

"Through the weekend, I think. They don't seem to be doing any more bird-watching, though. This morning they mentioned visiting Pennsylvania Dutch country. They had some travel pamphlets with them at breakfast. They seem to be planning what to do from day to day."

"They seem like such a nice couple," Alice mused, "but she appeared to be sad when she first arrived."

"She was very upset that her daughter is going away for college when the fall term starts. She was dreading having an empty nest. She's been more upbeat the last couple of days. Maybe she's come to terms with the change in her life."

"We were so fortunate that Father supported our decisions about what we wanted to do with our lives. I know it was hard on him when Louise left to study music and even harder when his baby wanted to flex her wings."

"He was so proud when you got your nursing degree, but I don't think he was excited about having a chef in the family."

"Of course he was. He wanted all of us to use the talents God gave us, but he never tried to dictate what we should do. I can still remember a sermon he gave when I was home from college. It praised Martha, even though it was Mary who sat at the Lord's feet to learn."

"I don't remember that one, but then I was young, and my mind wandered during church services."

"Well, you're focused now. Speaking of that, I wonder whether Joanna has done all her work the way she was supposed to. Cynthia hasn't seemed very pleased with her."

"Yes, our niece hasn't been her usual cheerful self," Jane agreed. "Something is troubling her, and Joanna seems to be the cause. I'm glad she's getting away from work, and Joanna, this afternoon."

"Where should I put Joanna's letter?" Alice asked. "She's been so eager to get it. I wouldn't want to misplace it."

"I'll take it upstairs and slide it under the door of her room," Jane volunteered, "but I don't think she's there. I can usually tell when a room is occupied, if only because the floor creaks or the water runs."

"Well, she'll return in her own good time. Somehow, when she's not here I worry about her. She's such a dreamer. I can just imagine her wandering into the country and not knowing the way back. I know that she's a grown-up, but somehow I feel responsible for her."

"Dear Alice," her sister said, laughing. "You've gone from rescuing baby animals to taking stray poets under your wing."

Chapter Fifteen

Cynthia drove as she and her mother made their way through the hilly Pennsylvania countryside, enjoying the bright green of new foliage and the occasional splash of color where wildflowers grew along the narrow road.

"I stopped in at the Acorn Antique Shop because they had a beautiful quilt in the window," Cynthia said. "Mrs. Holzmann is certainly nice. She told me about a gallery for homemade quilts in Three Oaks. It's only a tiny town, but they turned an abandoned corset factory into a place to display and sell local handcrafts and art. She said the prices are extremely reasonable and quilters from all over the state bring things to show and sell."

"You can take her word that it's worth the trip. Rachel and Joseph Holzmann are always helpful. Our town is lucky to have them in our midst."

"Well, it's a lovely day for a ride whether I find anything or not."

"I'm not clear on exactly what you want," Louise said.

"I'm hoping to find a quilt for my bed. I want to give my bedroom the warm, country look that the inn has. Being back and seeing what Aunt Jane has done with the bedrooms has inspired me to try something cozier in my apartment."

"That sounds lovely," Louise said enthusiastically.

It felt wonderful to be on an excursion with her daughter, and finishing jury duty had made her lighthearted with relief. Later she might question the jury's decision or think of other things she should have considered, but for today, she only wanted to enjoy the freedom that comes after completing a difficult task.

"There are so many quaint little towns tucked away in the Pennsylvania hills," Cynthia said. "It would take a lifetime of traveling to see every one. Are you sure we made the right turn at the last intersection?"

"Yes, according to the map, we should reach Three Oaks any minute now."

"I wouldn't want to get lost in these hills. So many twists and turns." Suddenly Cynthia laughed. "Can you imagine Joanna loose around here? She gets lost between her apartment and work."

Louise saw that Cynthia made a quick transition from the smile that had followed her laughter to a frown. She suspected that Cynthia was now thinking more somber thoughts of Joanna.

"There it is, right up ahead," Cynthia said.

Three Oaks had the look of a rural village. As they went down the main and only business street, they could see old neighborhoods on the side streets. Two-storied frame homes were set back from the street with lawns fenced or marked off with flower beds. Most houses had front porches that invited visits from the neighbors.

The main street had a pharmacy, a branch bank, a hardware store and a few other businesses, but for every building that was occupied, it seemed that one sat vacant.

"Life can't be easy in small places like this," Cynthia said. "Wouldn't it be nice if all the dying towns got a big influx of people from overcrowded megacities, sort of evening things out?"

"I love life in Acorn Hill, but you are right, not all small towns are as blessed as ours," Louise said thoughtfully. "Our people are able to find jobs in Potterston, but there's no larger town close enough to give employment to the people here."

"I wonder what they do."

"Probably things that serve the farming community," Louise guessed.

"Of course, you're right. It's easy to forget how many people make a living from the land. I always have a hard time imagining how it must feel to depend on the weather for crops. A farmer's life makes mine seem so easy."

Finding the arts and crafts center was not too difficult, thanks to roadside signs and arrows. It was housed in the huge former factory. The brick outer walls had once been painted but had faded to a dull gray with only a few streaks of color where the company name had been. Narrow slits served for windows. It was far from an inviting building from the outside, but those in charge had erected a yellow and green striped awning over the entrance to make it more welcoming.

A heavyset man with bright red cheeks presided over a

checkout counter just inside the entrance. He apparently took it as part of his job to give a capsule history of the building.

"Ladies used to wear those big, stiff corsets, you know." He pointed at an old-fashioned advertising card under glass on the counter. It showed a woman with an incredibly small waist wearing one of the company's products. "They used whale bone to make them. Not so different from a suit of armor." He laughed at the comparison.

"We'd like to look at the quilts," Cynthia said.

He wasn't through with his history lesson.

"I tell you, this was a booming town in my great-great-granddaddy's day. He sold Three Oaks corsets all the way to Philly and Pittsburgh, even went as far as Cleveland and Detroit in boom times. And he was only one of a whole army of salesmen. Of course, women quit wearing them by the twenties. They made umbrellas here for a while, then plastic rain hats and coats, but they never sold like the good old corsets. Last thing they tried here had something to do with foam rubber. Never did get exactly what, but the owner went bankrupt pretty quick."

"That's too bad," Cynthia said. "Thanks for the history of the building. I think we'll just look around, if you don't mind."

"Watch your step when you go up to the second floor. The stairs are pretty steep," he warned.

The walls were mostly bare brick while the floors were made of wide, wooden boards worn down from many years of use. The main floor was roughly partitioned, mostly by cases or shelving, and modern lighting displayed the crafts to good advantage. The building seemed even more massive from the inside than it appeared from the outside. Louise was amazed at the variety of handmade goods on display.

"Rachel didn't exaggerate about how big this place is," Cynthia said. "I hardly know where to begin looking. Do you want to start on the second floor and work our way down?"

"That sounds like a good plan," Louise said. "Lead the way."

They soon found that a large section of the second floor was devoted entirely to quilts. A middle-aged woman in jeans and a flowered blouse was hanging a quilt toward the end of the big open space.

"Can I help you with anything?" she asked with a friendly smile.

"I'm hoping to find a quilt for my bed," Cynthia said, "but I'm a bit overwhelmed by all the choices."

"Would you like me to walk you through some of the patterns?" she asked. "My husband and I manage this department, and I've been quilting for nearly twenty years."

"That would be wonderful," Cynthia said.

"Here's one of my favorite patterns," she said, pointing to a complex design with red, gold and royal blue dominating the color scheme. "It's called a medallion quilt, and it's one of the oldest patterns still used. English quilt makers brought the design to this country. See how it begins with a central motif and works out from the middle."

"It's lovely, but it doesn't fit my color scheme," Cynthia said.

"I always get a kick out of crazy patchworks like this," their guide said, pointing out another quilt. "It would go with almost everything because it has nearly every color in it. One theory is that the Japanese introduced the idea of mixing silks and velvets at the Centennial Exposition of 1876 in Philadelphia, and it became wildly popular to make them. Most folks think that thrifty homemakers just needed to make every bit of cloth count for something."

"This one especially appeals to me," Louise said, admiring a quilt with all the diverse scraps of material tied together by metallic threads that suggested a spider's web.

"Here's an all-time favorite design," the woman said. "It's the double wedding ring. It was especially popular during the Depression years when people could turn small scraps of colored cloth into a work of art."

"Look at the way the rings intersect," Cynthia said in awe. "I can't imagine cutting and sewing all those tiny pieces, not to mention forming perfect circles."

"Here's a design that I have on my bed. It's grandmother's flower garden, another favorite of the 1930s quilting revival. It's all hand sewn."

They circled around the area, looking at the huge array of quilts, but Louise wasn't surprised when Cynthia returned to the grandmother's flower garden. Each individual segment was edged in bright blue with yellow, pink, green and peach among the many colors used on a white background.

"I think this is the one," she said, checking out the price discreetly placed near the bottom. "It's a bit more than I'd hoped to pay, but it's a wonderful piece and worth the price considering how long it must have taken to make it."

"I'll be getting a check for two weeks of jury duty," Louise said. "I can't think of anything better to do with it. It won't pay for the quilt but it will help make the dent in your budget a bit smaller."

Cynthia protested, but Louise insisted that she wanted something good to come from her term of service.

"Whenever I visit you, I'll be reminded of how difficult it is to judge others."

After the quilt was layered in tissue and put in a large plastic bag, Cynthia thanked her mother profusely and expressed her appreciation to the saleswoman for her explanations about patterns. She led the way down creaky steps to the main floor.

"Be careful, Mother."

Louise smiled at her daughter's solicitude, but she did hang on to the railing.

Cynthia chatted happily about the quilt as they left, but Louise couldn't shake the feeling that something was on her mind. She thought of asking Cynthia if anything was bothering her, then decided Cynthia would tell her in her own good time.

"I'm famished," Louise said. "Shall we have lunch here?"

"Great! My treat. But where can we go? This town doesn't look very promising for restaurants."

"You might be surprised," Louise said. "Sometimes these

little towns have cafes or diners with wonderful home cooking. Jane taught me that. Don't judge a restaurant by the location."

"Well, let's test her theory." Cynthia pulled into the angle parking on the main street and pointed at a sign on the opposite side.

"The Tearoom," Louise read. "Worth a try."

The small restaurant was nearly deserted, but that wasn't necessarily a bad sign. It was well past the traditional lunch hour. There were small tables running the length of the long, narrow building, and the owners had decorated it with country crafts hanging on the walls, including a quilt that Louise recognized as a medallion design. Cynthia headed toward a table that offered a nice view of the street.

They read the small card that served as a menu and waited for several minutes without seeing anyone. Just when Louise was starting to wonder if the restaurant was open for business, a tiny elderly woman in a saffron and brown uniform came to the table and asked to take their order.

Louise ordered chicken à la king on a homemade biscuit, and Cynthia decided on lobster salad on a croissant. While they waited for their order, they indulged in sampling a delightful array of relishes and flavored butters on crispy homemade crackers.

"Aunt Jane was right," Cynthia said with a little grin.

"Indeed she was. If our meals are as tasty as these appetizers, I'll be very pleased."

When their orders arrived, they were delighted to see that the food was handsomely arranged on delicate flowered china.

Louise's dish was decorated with curls of pimento, while Cynthia's sandwich was accompanied by a slice of spiced apple and a small bunch of green grapes.

They spoke of casual things as they did justice to what turned out to be a lovely luncheon. They both passed on dessert even though the tray of pastries that the waitress presented was very tempting.

While she'd seemed to enjoy the luncheon, Cynthia allowed her mood to grow pensive when they got back to the car.

"Is something wrong?" Louise finally asked as they buckled up.

"Yes and no."

"Not an answer."

"It's Joanna. She just isn't suited to be an editor."

"I have to admit that I've wondered about her aptitude for the job."

"At first I was worried that she had blown all chance of getting the promotion, but now I've been notified that she's going to be fired."

Louise felt sad but didn't know what to say.

"Her work is a disaster. She tried to change the book she was editing into an entirely different work, one that doesn't suit our publishing aims at all. She has the author up in arms and threatening to return her advance. The art department is furious because her editing changed the focus of the illustrations and the printer needs her book immediately. Marketing is refusing to work with her—well, you get the picture."

"That bad?"

"Worse. She's getting two weeks' severance pay, but they want her out now. I'm afraid I volunteered to break the news to her."

"Oh dear."

"I like her, I really do," Cynthia said in a weary voice. "I'm not that much older than she, but I feel responsible for her as if she were my little sister. I was hoping that a quiet stay in Acorn Hill would help her concentrate on work, but she's hopeless. I didn't want her to walk into our newly renovated offices only to learn that she's out. I want to save her the humiliation of having to clear her desk and leave in front of everyone, but I can't tell you how much I don't want to be the one to tell her."

"It was sweet of you to offer."

"Offering is the easy part. Now I have to figure out when and how."

"What will she do?"

"I've no idea. She barely manages on her salary. Housing is so expensive around Boston that she'll probably have to give up her apartment. She would hate going back to her parents in Maine. I've even thought of letting her stay with me until she finds another job, but she wouldn't be an easy roommate. I only have the one bedroom, and there's absolutely no place for her things. You have no idea what a large library she has."

"I can imagine."

Louise felt terrible for Joanna and almost as sorry for Cynthia. Her daughter was kindhearted, but was there really anything else she could do for Joanna?

"Oh well." Cynthia sounded despondent. "I'll manage somehow. I can't imagine that it will come as a surprise. I did talk to her about the problems surrounding her work. Joanna has to know that she's badly botched the job."

Louise wasn't sure about that. In many ways, Joanna was like a child, delighted with everything she accomplished and oblivious to the reactions of others. She remembered how Alice had tried to discourage her from continuing with the library program. Joanna had flat out refused to be dismissed.

"As you know, dear, things have a way of working out. From what I've observed, Joanna is very resilient." Louise prayed that this ability of Joanna's to bounce back would continue to remain strong.

Chapter Sixteen 

Jane was humming to herself when Louise came down for breakfast Saturday morning.

"You sound cheerful," Louise said. "Is there some particular reason?"

"I was just planning dinner in my head. I thought we could celebrate the end of your jury duty by having a special meal."

"That sounds nice, although all your meals are special."

"Well, I plan to outdo myself. After all, Cynthia and Joanna will be leaving Monday, so what better time for a celebration?"

"Sounds lovely."

Louise tried to sound enthusiastic, but she was worried about Joanna's loss of her job. So far neither Jane nor Alice knew about it, and she'd agreed with her daughter not to mention the firing until Cynthia had a chance to tell Joanna. It was unlike Cynthia to procrastinate, but they both agreed that Sunday evening was soon enough. There was no harm in letting her enjoy the weekend at Grace Chapel Inn before hearing the bad news.

"I asked Ross and Margo Wallace to join us. I thought dinner would be a nice send-off for them. And, of course, Aunt Ethel is coming. She got along with them very nicely the last time they were together."

Louise smiled and nodded agreement even though her heart wasn't in Jane's plans.

"What can I do to help?"

"Not a thing. Spend the day with Cynthia."

"Have you told Joanna about dinner?"

"If there's one thing I've learned about her, it's not to assume anything, even that she'll show up for meals. I made a special point of asking her to join us this evening before she left the inn."

"I wonder where she goes all the time."

"Oh, she hangs out at the library or spends time talking to Viola. That reminds me, I'll invite Viola. That way Joanna will feel that she has a special friend at dinner, and it will be a small repayment for the time Wendell has spent at Viola's home. Let's see, that's nine people for dinner. I think I'll run over to the supermarket in Potterston. Would you mind watching the inn for me? I think the guest who came to visit her grandchildren will be checking out before noon. Alice has gone walking with Vera."

"I'll be happy to, but are you sure there's nothing I can do to help with dinner?"

"Not a thing."

Louise watched her sister leave armed with a detailed list and a pleased smile. She was glad Cynthia had decided to hold back on delivering the bad news. It would spoil the party for Jane if she knew that Joanna was being sacked.

Jane was in her element as she began the lengthy preparations for dinner. The appetizer she chose was baked salmon. Jane put the lovely fillet in the freezer for a short time in order to cut it into neat, thin slices. Then she marinated it for four hours in a blend of olive oil, lemon juice and dill. She would bake it for a short time just before calling her guests to the table. She washed and refrigerated sprigs of fresh dill to use as garnish and mixed a sauce of pasteurized egg, lemon juice, grated onion, finely cut dill and sour cream to drizzle over the fish.

For the main course, she planned individual fillets of beef in Madeira sauce. She would pan sear the meat at the last minute and set it aside, while she made the sauce using the meat drippings from the pan. Now she chopped the shallots and mushrooms for the sauce, covered them and set them on the counter. She planned a family favorite for the starch, scalloped potatoes, and for the vegetable, fresh asparagus. Her potato recipe was rich and delicious and called for two-plus hours in the oven, so she quickly peeled the potatoes, sliced them thin in her food processor and layered them with a cheese mixture. Then she poured rich cream over the potatoes, covered the dish with foil and placed the dish in the oven.

The meal cried out for a tangy finish, so she made a double batch of lemon squares. Such preparations might tire out another woman, but working in her kitchen on a family party was Jane's idea of a perfect day. She hummed—albeit a bit off key—as she tidied the kitchen after her preparations were finished. She was smiling as she climbed the stairs to her room to rest before dressing for dinner.

Cynthia asked her mother to join her for a walk, and Louise readily agreed. Time spent with her daughter seemed even more precious now that her departure was approaching.

Louise sometimes thought of living in Boston to be close to Cynthia, but in her heart she knew that big-city life was no longer for her. She thanked the Lord every day for the love of her sisters and the challenges of running the inn and instructing her music pupils.

"Joanna doesn't have a clue that she's in trouble," Cynthia said as they walked briskly down Hill Street toward Village Road, where they could really stretch their legs. "She's such a deep thinker when it comes to poetry, but sometimes she's oblivious to what's happening around her."

"I guess we have to love her for what she is. You can't really change people, you know."

"She's been acting peculiar—even for her. She's like a wind-up toy with the spring taut, all energy and movement without any progress."

"Well, you made the right decision not to tell her until the last minute. She does seem to enjoy talking poetry with Viola, and I understand that she's made a nest for herself in the library reading room," Louise said.

"Yes, but I would like to know what goes through that mind of hers. She's quite intelligent. How can she possibly not know that a company won't put up with her idiosyncratic behavior forever, particularly when it affects the quality of her work?"

Louise sighed. She didn't have an answer to give her daughter.

Alice made the dining room her top priority after Jane refused her help in the kitchen. She dusted and polished until the lovely old room was gleaming, and then set the table according to Jane's instructions. She used a pale pink linen tablecloth, the best china and crystal. In the middle of the table, she placed the flower arrangement that Jane had done. The deep pink peonies and purple lilacs not only provided color, but they also perfumed the room with their appealing scents. Finally, she put pink-and-lavender hand-dipped candles in crystal holders and placed them on either side of the flower arrangement. She stepped back and admired the total effect. She loved puttering around the inn, and enjoyed the beauty and comfort of her home. But she had to admit to herself that it would be good to get back to work on Monday.

After her chores were done, Alice went to her room and showered. She decided to dress up for Jane's special dinner. After a review of her choices, she selected a pale lime sheath with a matching short-sleeved jacket in a linen-like fabric. When she came downstairs, she found family and guests gathered in the parlor. She smiled when she saw that everyone else had chosen to dress up as well. The ladies all looked very festive in bright colors and prints, and Mr. Wallace was dapper in a blue blazer and gray slacks, but it was Joanna who took Alice by surprise. She had abandoned her usual uniform of a long skirt and casual knit top and was wearing a lovely silk suit in a fetching shade of peach. The fitted jacket and pencil skirt flattered her slender shape. She wore beige high heels that emphasized her shapely legs. It was almost as though she'd morphed into an entirely different creature. Given her indifference to food and her poor attendance at meals, Joanna provided a pleasant surprise by dressing up, and Alice was pleased to see the transformation.

Louise looked around the table after leading the gathering in a blessing, pleased by the celebratory atmosphere. Conversation had started up again immediately after the prayer. Guests and family engaged in lively banter. Louise smiled when she noticed Jane's skirt with yellow cats frolicking on a brown background. It reminded her that Wendell would be coming home after Joanna left. She missed the rascal and would be glad to see him patrolling about the inn again.

Mr. and Mrs. Wallace shared their vacation experiences with Ethel. Viola and Joanna seemed to have an unending store of literary topics to discuss, and Cynthia gracefully divided her time between her mother and her aunts. The meal was delicious and much appreciated by those gathered around the table. When the dishes had been cleared for dessert, Viola cleared her throat as an attention getter.

"I think this would be a good time for your news," she said to Joanna.

Suddenly the room was quiet, and all eyes were on the young poet, whose cheeks were unusually flushed and whose eyes sparkled.

"I do have good news," she said.

"Wonderful news," Viola prompted.

"A few months ago I interviewed for a teaching fellowship at a little college in Maine," Joanna told them. "The reason I did was that one of the professors was a judge in a poetry contest I won last year. She encouraged me to try for the position."

"It would be a wonderful opportunity to devote herself more fully to poetry," Viola said enthusiastically.

"At the beginning of March I got a letter saying that I was one of the two finalists, and that I would get their decision by the middle of April. I told them that I could be contacted here. Well, you can imagine how nervous I was when the fifteenth came and went with no news. Then, finally, a letter arrived."

"She got the fellowship!" Viola couldn't have sounded more excited if she had been named to the position herself.

Everyone around the table offered congratulations. Louise glanced at Cynthia and saw a delighted smile on her face.

"We've just gone through a college hunt with our daughter," Ross explained. "If it's complicated to be admitted as a regular student, I can only imagine what the fellowship process must be."

"I never thought of a career as a college teacher, but this sounds so appealing. I'll be able to teach a class on the nineteenth-century romantic poets. I'm already thinking of graduate work when my two-year contract expires. This might put me in line for a teaching fellowship at a university."

"It's so exciting I had to bite my tongue to keep from blurting it out," Viola said. "I've read many of Joanna's poems, and I've become her biggest fan."

"There is one thing." Joanna looked at Cynthia, her face filled with concern. "I will have to quit my job. I know that I should give notice, but there's so much to do, give up my apartment, sell my furniture—what there is of it—find housing near the college. And my mother finally approves of what I'm doing, maybe for the first time ever. She insists that I spend some time with the family this summer, which works out well because I'll be teaching only a hundred or so miles from home. But about my job—"

"I'll take care of it," Cynthia promised. "You don't even have to come to the office when we get back to Boston unless there are things in your desk that you need to take."

"Nothing at all. I was hoping so hard that I'd be picked that I took all my personal things home before we came here. Do you really think it would be all right if I didn't show up? I've tried to do everything that needed doing."

"I'm sure it won't be a problem."

Louise caught her daughter's eye and smiled. Cynthia shook her head with an expression only her mother could read. There was no reason to deliver the bad news that Joanna had lost her position with the publisher.

"We have something to say too," Ross said after Joanna had answered a spate of questions about her new position. "In fact, we have a gift for you, Ethel."

"For me?" Her face glowed as the group's attention shifted to her.

He took a small gift-wrapped box from his jacket pocket and handed it across the table to her.

"Shall I open it?"

"Please do," Margo said.

Everyone watched in silence as Ethel carefully removed the silver wrapping and opened a small velvet box.

"Why it's lovely!" She held up a small golden locket inset with a tiny yellow gemstone. "I don't understand."

"The locket is our way of saying thank you," Margo said. Ethel still looked totally perplexed, although she managed to thank them.

"You told Ross how hard it was for you when your youngest child left home, but you and your husband realized that you still had each other. The two of you were still together as you had been at the beginning of your marriage. Raising children hadn't changed that," Margo said.

"Yes, I remember."

"Well, Ross told me about your conversation, and I realized that this was my Penny's time to look for her own future. It's going to be hard on me, but I'm not alone."

"I'm going to miss our daughter too," Ross said, "but I tried to cover it up when I should have been sharing my feelings. When you told me about your husband, I realized that I had to admit to Margo how I felt."

"We haven't been bird-watching this week," Margo said a bit shyly.

"No, we've been hunting for something more important."

"I guess you could say we've been recapturing the closeness and companionship that we had at the beginning of our marriage,"

Margo said. "I realize now that an empty nest isn't the end of the world. In fact, it's just one more step in our journey through life. I'm so blessed to have a husband like Ross."

"And I intend to be a better one than I have been," he said. "The bottom line is that you helped open our eyes, Ethel. We hope you enjoy the locket."

"I love it," Ethel said, tears forming in her pale blue eyes.

She got up from her place at the table and went over to Margo, enveloping her in a hug.

On Sunday afternoon, Cynthia, her mother and aunts were enjoying the beautiful spring day on the front porch. Joanna was off with Viola, and the Wallaces had left that morning for home.

"I'm going to miss Margo and Ross," Jane said. "They knew so much interesting bird lore. For example, did you know that cowbirds lay their eggs in warbler nests and expect the other birds to care for the cowbird chicks?"

"No, I never heard of that," Alice said.

"Nor I," said Louise. "I wonder why the warblers don't just push the intruders' eggs out of the nest."

"Ah, Louise, you are right on," Jane said. "Scientists wondered the same thing and discovered that if a warbler did that, the cowbird would come back and destroy the warbler's eggs and nest."

"The ruffians!" Louise exclaimed, much to the amusement of Cynthia and her aunts.

"Speaking of birds and nests," Cynthia said, "I have to

admit that at first I thought Margo's reaction to her daughter's leaving was a bit over the top. However, I'm suddenly feeling like an empty-nester myself. I really will miss Joanna. I got used to taking care of her."

"Yes," Alice said. "Having someone leave abruptly who was a part of your life is difficult. I remember how sad Father, Louise and I were when Jane went off to art school."

"And I was bereft when you went off to college," Louise said to Cynthia, patting her hand. "But it's the normal pattern of life. And it really is a wonderful event when the fledgling flies off on her own."

Jane raised her glass of iced tea. "Here's to Joanna and the Wallaces' daughter and all the baby birds of spring. May God keep all of them in His loving protection."

Jane was answered by a chorus of heartfelt amens. Spontaneously, Louise softly began to sing the refrain of a favorite hymn, and Cynthia joined in:

I sing because I'm happy,
I sing because I'm free,
For His eye is on the sparrow,
And I know He watches me.

As the last notes of their sweet song faded, contentment reigned at Grace Chapel Inn.

Jane's Orange Blossom Baklava

MAKES ABOUT THIRTY PIECES

SYRUP:

2 ½ cups sugar
1 cup water
2 tablespoons lemon juice
2 tablespoons orange blossom water
(available in specialty stores or online)

Dissolve sugar in water and lemon juice, and simmer until syrup thickens enough to coat a spoon. Add orange blossom water and simmer for two minutes, stirring constantly. Allow to cool and then chill in refrigerator.

PASTRY:

1 pound phyllo dough
(usually in grocery freezer case)
½ pound unsalted butter, melted
1 ½ cups pistachios, walnuts or
almonds, coarsely chopped
2 ½ tablespoons sugar

Preheat oven to 350 degrees. Use a pastry brush to apply some of the butter to the sides and bottom of a 9x13-inch baking pan. Place half of the pastry sheets (phyllo dough) in the pan, one at a time, brushing each sheet with butter, including the top one. Fold the sheets to fit the pan as necessary. While you are working, keep the sheets from drying out by covering with a damp tea towel.

In a small bowl, mix the nuts and sugar, and distribute evenly over the pastry sheets in the pan. Follow the same procedure as above with the rest of the pastry sheets.

Using a sharp knife, cut the pastry diagonally into elongated diamond shapes (about three inches long and two inches wide).

Bake at 350 degrees for thirty minutes, then raise the temperature to 450 degrees and bake another fifteen minutes. The pastry should be puffed and a light golden color. Remove the pastry from oven and immediately pour the cold syrup over it. Let cool.

When ready to serve, use a sharp knife to go over the cuts in the pastry and remove to individual plates or a serving platter.

About the Authors 

Pam Hanson and Barbara Andrews are a daughter-mother writing team. They began working together in the early 1990s and have had twenty books published, including fifteen under the pseudonym Jennifer Drew.

Pam has taught reporting courses at West Virginia University and is now director of advising for the School of Journalism. She has presented writing workshops and has been involved in school and church activities. She lives with her husband, a professor, and their two sons in West Virginia, where she shares her home with her mother.

Previous to their partnership, Barbara had twenty-one novels published under her own name. She began her career writing Sunday school stories and contributing to antiques publications. Currently she writes a column and articles about collectible postcards. For more than twenty years she has sponsored a mail postcard sale with all proceeds going to world hunger relief. She is the mother of four and the grandmother of seven.

Tales from Grace Chapel Inn

Recipes & Wooden Spoons
by Judy Baer

Hidden History
by Melody Carlson

Ready to Wed
by Melody Carlson

The Price of Fame
by Carolyne Aarsen

We Have This Moment
by Diann Hunt

The Way We Were
by Judy Baer

The Spirit of the Season
by Dana Corbit

The Start of Something Big
by Sunni Jeffers

Spring Is in the Air
by Jane Orcutt

Home for the Holidays
by Rebecca Kelly

Eyes on the Prize
by Sunni Jeffers

Summer Breezes
by Jane Orcutt

Tempest in a Teapot
by Judy Baer

Mystery at the Inn
by Carolyne Aarsen

Saints Among Us
by Anne Marie Rodgers

Keeping the Faith
by Pam Hanson
& Barbara Andrews

Never Give Up
by Pam Hanson
& Barbara Andrews

Sing a New Song
by Sunni Jeffers

Rally Round the Flag
by Jane Orcutt

Prayers and Pawprints
by Diann Hunt

Once you visit the charming village of Acorn Hill, you'll never want to leave. Here, the three Howard sisters reunite after their father's death and turn the family home into a bed-and-breakfast. They rekindle old memories, rediscover the bonds of sisterhood, revel in the blessings of friendship and meet many fascinating guests along the way.